LOUIS' PREOCCUPATION WITH NAPOLEON-CAESAR

LOUIS' PREOCCUPATION WITH NAPOLEON-CAESAR

by

Michael Ulysses Gilbert

Quantity Purchases:
Companies, professional groups, clubs, and other organizations may qualify for special terms when ordering quantities of this title. For information, email info@ebooks2go.net, or call (847) 598-1150 ext. 4141. www.ebooks2go.net

Published in the United States by eBooks2go, Inc.
1827 Walden Office Square, Suite 260, Schaumburg, IL 60173

ISBN: 978-1-5457-6040-6

Library of Congress Cataloging in Publication

Table of Contents

"Where am I?"

Where am I, and why does my body lie so still? I awoke though only to find my movements restrained. For even the lids of my eyes won't open themselves from some untold force. I have tried to sit up, but only failed as those same attempts failed to roll my body from one side to the other as well. What thing is this which has now befallen upon me and whose strength have I now encountered capable enough to render my body so incapacitated?

Am I paralyzed? Please dear god, not that! Don't leave me stuck in some chair or this bed for the remainder of my life as some motionless, impractical invalid!

Wait a minute… I think I just moved my head up and down through all that hysteria. Yes, I can move my head up and down, and my neck moves right along with it. What about turning my head from left to right? All right and I can do that too! Only trying to sit up still proves useless. Maybe that's the only movement I am left with from my head to my neck. Only how could this be, and why are my hands so cold?

Cold…my hands are so cold. Yes cold! A paralyzed man cannot feel cold and my fingers. Yes, and I can move all ten fingers, yet still, I cannot move my wrists to bring warmth to the fingertips of my cold hands. By whose authority holds my wrists against this cold bed? Keeping me idle against my will?

Maybe I can stand? Perhaps my upper body doesn't completely work, but maybe my legs do? Though I'll have to use all the strength from my lower body to compensate for my weaker upper body. Now, I can bend my knees, though only slightly. For now my ankles appear to be restricted as much as my wrists do. I guess that question has been answered as well.

Only now what has become of me, and where am I and that light? Where is that light coming from? For it must be so bright on the other side for even my closed eyes can behold its brightness. Only the strange light doesn't seem to wake me as I feel so tired and ready to go back inside my sleep once more. How long have I been asleep? Sleep… yes sleep…

Aah! My dream…coming back to me that wonderful, beautiful creation. Giving back what belongs to me. With her perfection! Her lingering scent which gently hovers over me. Only whose scent are you? The one I have known only a short time ago or one whose appearance I have known from throughout my brief existence? Who wears fleshly temptations day and night? Arousing my every capable instinct inside and out or whose delicate skin glows from the sweet smell of your sweat clinging onto your naked flesh?

Yes, I believe that is where my dream left me. Upon a wealth of virginal scent slowly emitting from the two fingers I gracefully slide inside her vaginal warmth. Her bosom firm with an insatiable desire and her want for more. More when soon she finds herself entirely awakened, surrendering herself wholly inside my impromptu love. Her stomach rising with temptation while slowly lowering with the anticipation of further seduction. Her breath whispering back to me. Softly, she lies upon me. Pure as untouched waters that are yet to be polluted by any man. Whereupon the zenith of her euphoria, she cries out to me.

"Yes, it is me. I as now as I am always. Yes Louis. Yes!"

When suddenly, her maternal love would soon take over. Reducing my limbs while yielding onto her own. Opening myself to her will as she now lay firmly against me. Establishing herself against my submission as she slowly comes into me. Announcing herself to me as I hold her from beneath me.

"Oh, goddess from above never leave. Never leave nor forsake me."

"No Louis. No! This I shall never do."

"Then yes. Come into me continually and speak to me always!"

"Louis Ney"

"Good morning. Nurse Monroe. I see we have a new patient with us today."

"Good morning doctor. Yes, this is Mr. Louis Ney. He came in last night just as the third shift was arriving."

"Well, it looks as if this Mr. Ney was a handful." The doctor was only too quick to observe.

"He certainly was doctor. According to the night shift, Mr. Ney here, came in quite hysterical while on some rant about some creature. A snake, I believe it was. A snake he called Moloch to which remained constant at his side and never more than an earshot away, which is also why he was immediately brought to us. The night staff didn't waste any time restraining and sedating our new psych patient either.

"What did he come in for?"

"Don't you already know? This one is from the high school. You must have heard?"

"Hear what? No, I haven't heard a thing. However, I do hear that cup of coffee sitting on the counter next to you."

"Here you go doctor. Black just the way you like it."

"Thank you nurse and is it just me or is this room cold inside? Nurse, why don't you get our new patient another blanket."

"Right away, doctor, but as I was asking, have you truly not heard anything about this patient?"

"Nothing I'm aware of, although I did leave the jail earlier than usual yesterday. I wasn't feeling well and went straight to bed when I got home. Got up late this morning and rushed back to the jail. Fortunately, it was only some twenty-four-hour bug. Now, what's all this you are trying to tell me?"

"Well, anyway, doctor, it was all over the news. Isn't there even one blanket in here?"

"The orderlies are always changing things around in these rooms. I believe the blankets are further down. Anyway, you were saying nurse?"

"Oh yes, yesterday doctor. Over at the high school? Those two murders?"

"Two murders at the high school? What do you mean nurse?"

"It's what I've been trying to tell you. Two savage killings at our own Downers Grove High School, but the news reports really haven't said much more than that and you haven't heard any of this yet?" As she shot the doctor a curious look. "Haven't you read the night nurse's report?"

The doctor shook his head. "No, as I said before, I went home early and even slept through my alarm clock this morning."

"Finally, a blanket."

"Well, what else have you heard?"

"There was some information our night nurse passed along…"

"Alright nurse, I'm waiting."

"Well, it seems one of the officers who brought in Mr. Ney told our night nurse he was most definitely their prime suspect. There, that should keep him warm."

"Their prime suspect and…? And what nurse? I will read last night's entry in a minute."

"That's really about it. Although she did seem privy to another bit of information, albeit perhaps a little gossip."

"Oh, just go ahead nurse and quit beating around that bush. You and I know very well this town thrives around any kind of sensational gossip."

"Well anyway, I guess the police found our Mr. Ney here fast asleep on the floor of the woodshop over at the high school while then becoming quite irate once they had awakened him. Throwing himself about with fresh blood covering his body, then on some tirade of why he did what he did and for some empire, and a Miss Tolemy, who he kept repeating over and over. The night nurse even thought this Miss Tolemy was one of the teachers over there."

"Hmmm, that does make one wonder who his actual victims were? Has the news reported on any of this yet?"

"Not to my knowledge though like I said the news is reporting very little. It's unclear if the victims were students, teachers, or who they were. The only fact reported in the news is the two homicides. They did not even mention our new patient here or any other for that matter."

"Well, whoever those poor souls are, it's just incomprehensible. That big city mayhem has found its way to our once peaceful little town."

"It's too bad though Dr. Trumann. He's so young. I wonder why at his age?"

"Yes, though one has to wonder more for those poor families who have only begun to mourn."

"Well yes doctor. That is true enough. These families and what they must be going through right now. To lose their loved ones from such shocking and horrific circumstances as they have. I suppose I was only reflecting on the boy's youth. Anyway, three families will undoubtedly change forever now, and that is certainly more than too bad."

"Hmmm…"

"What is it doctor?"

"These notes from the third shift. I wonder if our Dr. Eichman even knows the term moderation? This amount of Haldol administered to our new patient seems more than excessive. Take a look nurse."

"Well of course you would know better than me. However, as I was saying before, the night nurse was explaining to me not only did he resist police over at the high school, but upon his immediate arrival here as well. She stated how the entire Downers Grove police department had to bring him in. I believe the second page of those notes will confirm much of what she told me."

"Yes, here it is page two. Thank you nurse, and have I complimented on your appearance yet this morning?"

"No you have not doctor, but I know you will."

"Alright then, on the floor of page two.... and after finding Mr. Ney on the floor at the school's woodshop, Mr. Ney then violently awoke resisting arrest and etcetera, etcetera.... Subsequently, the suspect was strapped onto the paramedic's gurney, then upon his arrival at the jail, he continued to proceed with more violent outbursts. Remaining unresponsive to police and other authoritative commands and etcetera, etcetera..."

"Do you see what I mean?"

"Yes, indeed I do Eva," the doctor now spoke from a more relaxed tone. "A new Fragrance as well?"

"Why yes doctor. I bought it just the other day."

"Very nice Nurse Monroe," he said before returning to his usual doctor demeanor.

"I see page three continues with our subject while describing his delusional carry-on. Apparently, Mr. Ney believes that a utopian state is in our near future. Some imperial dynasty with more delusionary preoccupation with none other than Napoleon and Caesar."

"Hmmm, almost intriguing though I'm beginning to now understand why our new patient is with us at the psych ward and not downstairs. Perhaps our good Dr. Eichman was correct after all."

"What about the part of his lover? Have you come to that yet? He claims one of the teachers over at the high school was once in love with him. Could it possibly be that Miss Tolemy, the name our night nurse overheard?"

"I highly doubt that. As if any teacher at the high school would ever be in love with this megalomaniac."

"It could happen. Who knows what goes on in schools nowadays?"

The doctor screwed up his nose with distaste. "I suppose it could, though I must interpret this as more delusional behavior. And what about this Napoleon and Caesar Fixation? Does he actually believe he is one of them or both of those war enthusiasts combined?"

He tapped a thoughtful finger at the report. "From these notes, it appears that he joins their two names together-Napoleon-Caesar. A first-rate personality disorder would be my first conclusion."

"Napoleon-Caesar hmmm ...?"

"More coffee doctor?"

"No thank you. I'm going to wrap things up here for now. In the meantime, keep our Mr. Louis Ney comfortable and loosen those straps a notch as well. I swear, sometimes those barbarians from third shift treat this place more like a medieval bastille than a modern hospital. Anyway, I'll come back to check on our new patient this afternoon. Perhaps then he'll be more responsive. By the way nurse, your hair? You have really outdone yourself once again."

"Why thank you doctor," Nurse Monroe nodded back with a smile.

"And good day to you doctor."

Voices. I hear voices. Only this voice is not inside, but from outside. Outside me. One speaking to another. I should think one female and the other male. If only I could open my eyes, then see whose voice surrounds me. See whose voice stands before me and discover where my body now lies. Only my eyes stay closed as my ears do as well as these same voices utter only sounds which my body cannot perceive. What thing is this which now leaves me so impaired? The voices. They done this thing to me. They paralyzed my sight, my senses, every movement. Only what monsters could leave me to only sleep and bound to never awake again? No, I must fight this sleep and leave this place before I never rise again! Only I'm still so very tired and my limbs ever so weak. Weak where only sleep wants to invade my body. Then come inside me If you wish as I cannot fight you any longer only give back my dream which belongs to me. Give back her licentious beauty she commands with her. Give back my dream!

Dream? Is that you? You who now speaks to me? Whose soft hands now touch me: Delivering my laden hands and wrists their relief? Only what dream are you who can seemingly cause my limbs to feel so much lighter? To what is this which now comes to pass? Wait…is it her? The woman's voice who now touches me and now my other hand? Yes, just maybe...yes, it is her! Whose warmth touches my cold skin. Only I wonder who she is and whose soft hands belong to such beauty as my dream before her. My dream. Yes, I remember now. I remember her...

Her warm touch permeates throughout my body as her flesh lies gently against me. For now her every shame is released and every pleasure is pursued. She who now lies before me. Who lives inside me.

Only what now? Her touch suddenly eludes me, and darkness intrudes my thoughts once more. Where are you going with my dream? Oh mistress of darkness don't leave me all alone. Alone and without you. Come back with my dream and deliver your smile again.

Only the dream did leave as the strange woman's benevolent touch ceased to relieve me. What has come to pass where such soft hands no longer relieve my limb's heavy burden?

Then I know what I shall do. I will loudly cry out to seek the mysterious woman's voice once more. Surely the strange woman will then come back. Come back to me.

"Cu, Cu, cum... com ba, baa, back, com... damn!" To those who render my lips without. For now only the sounds of broken words spill from my mouth and to my unknown host. Only why have you left me and all alone while taking my dream with you? You have no right to take that which is mine!"

Only I instinctively knew I was not alone. Her voice would never leave my side. It was mine. While she would never leave my side; naked with only my fears to accompany me, but the snake, Moloch...?

Moloch would leave my side without ever leaving at all. For it is a treacherous being and its powers are relentless and its commands unstoppable and absolute. Like the commanding bellows of an army drill instructor that are systematically obeyed by the mindless, robotic soldier marching in time — 'Right (left) step, march.'

Only where is she? What has become of my lover? What has happened to me?

"Miss Frenchie"

July tenth was the arrival of my ninth birthday and until now for the most part I have lived an abundant childhood. It was the beginning of my own curiosities where discoveries would abound.

Where upon the first big discovery would be that of the two lives I would naturally depend upon most... my mother and father. However, whose true identities would not reflect that of my own. Announcing their "arrangement" with me upon my seventh year where two models were presented to me though unlike from that of my own past. Two lives who dwell outside me. Where any sincere reflection of my actual birth and birth parents was carefully concealed from me save from their sole response to me, "Your mother and Father are no longer with us Louis. Sadly, that is all we know."

"Sadly," I would repeat under my breath as this same explanation would repeat itself back to me. Only they did not look "sadly." Only matter of fact in their response to me while always carefully selecting the very same words for my continued concealment. Hence, would I press the subject further to their greater annoyance.

No longer with us? Would I begin in my pursuit to their displeasure. Then perhaps they dwell elsewhere? Maybe inside another country. One you are not aware of from your own past or present time. Some place perhaps escaping you? Where?

Until one day they did explain further as my own curiosities would give way to their own impatience.

"No, no Louis! No! We have told you again and again where they are. They are not here. They are no longer with us nor do they exist in some other remote land or any other ruling Fatherland. No Louis. No, your mother and father are dead. They are dead. Dead Louis! Now go Louis. Run off and entertain yourself by some other means and forget this matter altogether!"

Dead. At last a meaning I could interpret more clearly. More defined in its ability to understand even from my innocent youth. Where one particular box and a single hole in the ground accounted for One's aftermath.

"Only why? Why were they dead?" Would I Keep asking myself and soon, I would entreat further along the nature of their demise.

"Why are they not here and why am I still here? Why have I escaped death? Why...?" And to this their agitation only grew, hence would I at last decide to pursue the matter no longer. For in time I could only assume they would tell me.

For I knew there was seemingly something more inside me to which perhaps they knew. A past my subconscious behavior wished to reveal. However, at the same time an apprehension, Perhaps I did not want to know. Where the truth lay dormant. For if this truth did lie at my subconscious then there has to be a reason, a purpose why my flesh was so willing to suppress any memories deep inside. Only I Knew one day my subconscious would talk to me. "One day," I told myself, "One day."

Despite the inevitable interest I had in my biological parents I continued to strengthen and grow from the due servitude my counterfeit parents would provide me. Feeding me, clothing and sheltering me. Protecting me from any unsound existence from all around, only unaware of the entity inside me.

Only how could they have known the parasite to which dwelled inside me? A creation from my brief existence. Breathing my every breath alongside mine...Emerging from within to never cease. Reappearing again and again.

Though still through these earlier enigmatic trials of my childhood I came to possess more beneficial outcomes. Qualities to which would prove themselves productive and pragmatic to the surroundings around me. Abilities my own youthful body demonstrated through both strength and agility from most boys my age. Realizing a superiority above them. While achieving an intelligence my own classmates looked up to. Realizing their own weaknesses from that of my own prowess. Though understanding the invaluable adolescent years now and ahead. While reflecting upon my own auspicious onset. My nurturing timeline into a future where more discoveries would unfold themselves to me.

One discovery I would immediately enjoy was that of my very first school girl crush. A love which would evolve with each and every school year. While from her others would follow.

Her name was Miss Frenchie, and she was my third-grade teacher. Though ignored by most boys who were smitten with much younger teachers whose diplomas had yet to gather any dust. However, Miss Frenchie was much older than that while observing her fortieth birthday come and go. Still she made the most impressionable appearance upon my boyhood gaze. With her warm dark skin and her soothing crystal green eyes staring back at me. No doubt the same kind of impression her first and only husband would have had some twenty years prior. However, those same number of years must also include the unfortunate length of time Miss Frenchie has been absent from her ill-fated husband as well. Where upon the most freakish accident, did her new groom succumb too. Walking hand and hand as new lovers do along the sunrising shores of some Louisiana Coast Miss Frenchie's only known love made one fatal step.

Although seemingly harmless the exposed foot of one hapless groom landed just enough onto the flesh of the one of many flying saucer-like jellyfish washed up onto the Louisiana shores. While these alien-like creatures presumingly all lie lifeless this particular one still possessed life and with its own departing life took another. Poor Mr. Frenchie never knew what struck him. Taken away more Suddenly than either could have imagined.

Despite her misfortune Miss Frenchie however quickly overcame her tragedy and with profound resilience pressed on with her now lone existence as the town's only third-grade teacher. For now her students became her only love and with every new class Miss Frenchie's most unusual and never changing proclamation would she entertain amongst her latest students. Beginning with her warm introduction, "Good morning third graders and welcome. My name is Miss Frenchie and I will be your third-grade teacher for the duration of this school year. Now our first order of business is to become familiar with each and every one of you. However, before I read off your names I would like to share a small portion from my very own family history," and from her own lips she began to proceed with her most peculiar though intriguing, declaration. "As your third grade teacher. I am also equally proud to disclose to all of you my family's extended past. One to which I can claim imperial descent and whose name you may have…"

But before any revered royalty could be announced, confused hands would quickly rise to overwhelm the teacher's own audacious proclamation.

"Impure? I think I heard that word in church," One girl would promptly confess from the front row, "but does that mean you're impure teacher?"

"No dummy, Miss Frenchie can't be impure," quickly quipped a boy next to her. "Didn't you just hear her say she was decent and my dad says the only friend you should have is a decent one."

"Imperial. My Family claims that too, but we claim ours on toast with grape jelly," proudly announced another student from the back row.

Now to be sure the family history of Miss Frenchie Seemed most unequal to that of her immediate peers and whether this was good or bad amongst the townspeople I could not be sure. For the only certainty I knew was the feeling I got from my nine-year-old body which seemed to resonate unexplainably whenever Miss Frenchie was anywhere near my presence. Although at the time I was told this was nothing unusual and even a common occurrence among boys of my age.

Now the story goes that Miss Frenchie can not only claim imperial descent but can draw a direct bloodline from herself today to that of none other than the emperor Napoleon Bonaparte of France himself. Exiled hundreds of miles from the shores of West Africa on the remote island of Saint Helena the Fallen emperor is said to have had a rather quaint relationship with one of the natives. There are some who even say she may have been a young slave girl.

Now as one could quite imagine this was not the type of publicity Napoleon and his entourage would have wanted to entertain and to make matters worse the young girl became pregnant. Now upon the revelation of this young girl's pregnancy and to avoid any embarrassment Napoleon swiftly seized the young girl from her family where she was then secretly lodged until her clandestine pregnancy was completed. However, tragedy struck at the unfortunate mother as it was said her young body was just too weak to live through her apparently troubled pregnancy, though a healthy baby girl was produced.

Once delivered Napoleon secretly gave up the child to an entirely new family. It was rumored the family of the deceased daughter rejected their new grandchild asserting Napoleon was nothing more than a rapist who murdered their beloved daughter. The newly chosen family was of the same poor peasantry and were coerced into secrecy by Napoleon regarding the child's true identity. Even so, local gossip was inevitable as this family of poor stock began to attain a sum of minor wealth as well as those who swear upon seeing the great emperor himself visiting the child's new home.

After the emperor's death in 1821 the girl remained with her adopted family and continued her existence On the remote British isle. At sixteen years of age she was married to her only husband until his death in 1840. Outliving him some twenty years. It was also said she had given birth to nine children from whom two tragically died. Whereas those children in turn married and had children of their own and so on and so forth until the family lineage reached its current generation to which Miss Frenchie now claims descent from.

Today it is said that well over one hundred descendants are able to claim this imperial line. Although intriguing, even for a nine year old, the story alone could not have aroused the sensations I felt around this noble empress. For inside my own virgin eyes Miss Frenchie was the most beautiful woman I had ever seen. Her dark skin shining amidst the afternoon sun, complementing her slender goddess like looks and streaming ebony hair.

Yes, to be sure Miss Frenchie was the most beautiful woman my youthful eyes had laid upon. While a most pleasant distraction in my everyday learning. Though still I continued to progress rather nicely in arithmetic and reading hoping Miss Frenchie would fall in love with the smartest boy in class. That and my unusual rate of growth as a grade school student, which I thought certainly would attract Miss Frenchie one day as well.

When soon I began to reflect more deeply upon these earlier accomplishments. I was one of the tallest boys in class and I knew I was a lot better looking than most of these undersized runts around me. I was just as smart too. For it would take more than two syllables to challenge my vocabulary while long division proved to be no match as well. This in turn had me thinking further still.

Maybe that Snake wasn't so clever after all? While although its appearance began to frequent my daily thoughts more and more I would still find control of my own intellectual will. While the physical strength of my flesh only continued to grow.

Though still I had to wonder. For how long was this thing going to continue inside me? For what purpose was it to serve? Was this the strength and intellect my flesh fed from? Whose tongue seemingly grew closer. While offering its continued chatter throughout me. It's prolific crafty illusions alongside me with only more thoughtless rhetoric toward me. What will become of this thing? This snakelike being? What...and again I asked what will become of me?

"Picture Day"

"Please sit quietly in your seats children and your eyes on me. Now these forms I am passing out need to be signed by your parents if all of you want to be in next week's class picture. Also make sure you bring them back by next Thursday or sooner because Friday Mr. Foster will be here with his camera."

"Alexander! Now what is so important that you had to turn around and start talking to Philip?"

"I was only telling Phillip how great it will be to gather all of us together into one picture. We will always be remembered!"

"Yes Alexander. That will be something. A great thing Alexander. No one will forget us or you."

Picture day! One of the most prized events in the entire school year & since my preschool days picture day has always given me the reverence I so deeply deserved. This due in part to my initial speedy growth of my youthful being, hence always the chosen student to stand immediately next to the latest of my yearly revolving teachers. Only this time would be much different, unlike previous picture days... where any teacher would do. Male or female, it wasn't an issue. Kind or mean spirited it just didn't matter. Even the prettier ones I remained indifferent towards. No, before was much different. For in those former times, I sought only after the teacher's higher social status inside the school. While this higher importance in turn led to my own elevated position, but not only for that one day, but for many years to come as that one picture would remain steadfast in time. For within this picture in time I became older, closer to a man and overall superior to my classmates. Only now.... now would be much different!

Sure I'll remain superior over the others, but this time I would stand side-by-side with my first real love. My lover whom someday would request my hand in eternal union.

Only I knew that day would have to wait. Wait until the side of her warm body touches against my own and then would we feel the whole of each other. For now only our hands have touched with the passing of assignments and graded materials, but now picture day draws near! Picture day will her slender shoulder brush against the side of my face as we stand not quite head to toe for after all I am still only nine years old. Then will the gentle reach of my lover's arm touch my shoulder while the warm flesh of my naked arm behold her maternal womanly waist and finally my unexplored hand will welcome her strong, fervent thigh.

Then will that day grant me my manhood. Will I throw away that little boy who's always tucked away from adult themes. Only what about Neil?

Neil? He must have jumped a foot if not more since last school year. Rats! What then will become of me? He will be amongst the chosen. He will stand beside my lover. He will see. She will come to know.

"Louis... Louis Can you hear me? It's me... Moloch."

"Yes of course I can hear you. Do you not live inside me? Only now go away. Go away! I have no time for you.

"No Louis, you know I cannot do that."

"Then stay if you wish, only I will not listen. Can you hear that?!"

"You know I love you and this business with Neil should not concern you. For Neil is nothing like you and I have given you everything while Neil comes without, but you and Miss Frenchie...Yes, you and her are one. But only through me. A creation of our coexisting trinity. Listen to me Louis and hear what I have to say."

What words now speak at me from the Snake's own dubious tongue? Miss Frenchie and I are nothing alike. My fair skin against her dark ebony tone while she is certainly much older than I. Then there is her fine accent from a collection of African, British, and French sounds which comprise her native land of Saint Helena. Clueless, Clueless are you. How is it I could come to believe in you? Such a vile, unreliable creature as you?" *"Because you are my flesh Louis and for this reason you pursue my counsel."*

"Only this time I shall not pursue. I was only too quick to assert on my behalf. For the Voice is my friend. One who abides inside my dreams. Whose maternal counsel watches over me, trustworthy and upright. Who gives only proper direction and without the worries and disruptions from those of your own treacherous tongue. Her lead shall I alone follow."

"Dummy! You are a real dummy aren't you Louis? You cannot abandon me without leaving her too. For I am her. That dream you so ardently desire each and every time you close your eyes. Dream I will continue to grant if only you adhere to my will. Do you not get this Louis or just perhaps you never will?"

"The Perfect Shot"

With Friday slowly drawing nearer I waited for that day to stand side by side with my teacher. My hopeful lover.

"Only will I stand next to her?" I repeatedly asked myself throughout the week or will another bump me off this highly sought after position amongst my class?

Neil finally grew up, though hopefully a little too late as I have been the sole one who has stood next to the teacher since my preschool days. I have stood taller than all the rest I told myself and it is there, where the cameraman's logic will take him as his keen eyes will arrange our class for yet another school year. Yes, I was the first. Sorry Neil. Besides, was it not the Snake who told me there was nothing to worry about? Who said Miss Frenchie and I are alike? That we are one and the same? An equal coexistence?

"Alright third graders, eyes up here. Now classroom we will now begin to quietly form a line in the hallway and then walk even quieter to the gymnasium. Mr. Foster will be patiently waiting for us." Miss Frenchie needed only to say his name when at last Friday was here! For it was Mr. Foster whose name was synonymous with every kind of photography in and around our small rural town. With a cloud of white hair his smile remained glued onto his portly appearance as if he was the one who was always receiving the camera's shot. Mr. Foster was so good at his trade he could direct each and every student down to their last quarter inch in height.

"Maggie you stand next to Scot, Jeremy you stand in front of Scot and you with the bushy red hair stand behind Maggie."

Now the teacher's placement always remained the same as he or she would stand tallest amongst our class. End of the back row and always standing to the right of his or her class. Likewise, my own hallowed spot among my fellow classmates had always been a sure thing, but today...would today be different?

"Neil," Mr. Foster abruptly shouted out. "Now what kind of daily bread has your mother been feeding you this past summer? Now you've grown an arm's length if not more. Louis, Kindly change places with Neil and Neil will you now have the honor to stand next to your teacher this year."

"No! Change places with Neil," I started to repeat back to myself. "No, have your eyes finally betrayed you?"

Only I knew better at the time and although not entirely unexpected I was still blown away with the audacity from the announcement delivered from our town's immortal photographer. Now I was sandwiched between a glorified Neil and some nobody. Now I was the fool like every other student who surrounded me, but not Neil. No, Neil will be noticed now. Neil will now stand upon the pedestal sitting firmly below his feet. Neil will exist amongst the trivial, insignificant remainder of us.

It was wrong. Wrong once again! Moloch who openly confessed Miss Frenchie and I were one and the same. Only I should have known better than to draw upon its counsel once more. Why I must be as dumb as it! I should have sought out only the dream and her prudent guidance from the beginning. She would have never allowed Neil to become my substitute or anyone else for that matter. She would have properly counseled me into sneezing on Neil's Tuesday lunch or warning Neil's bus driver of Neil's sudden attack with typhus. No, this cannot be for the teacher was mine and mine alone. It's a mistake! An injustice between Miss Frenchie and my own glorification.

Only the time had now come where it was too late as Mr. Foster was preparing himself for his most famous line comprising a mere two words...smile everyone!

Standing behind his tripod, Mr. Foster carefully set the camera dials then focusing one eye into the camera he would then take in one deep breath..."and three, two, one aannnn smile everyone annnn... wait a minute! Neil, it looks as if you forgot to comb your hair this morning. I was so impressed with your latest growing spree I seemed to have overlooked that unkempt hair of yours. Now come up here so I can properly address that tangled mess on top of your head."

Now Mr. Foster carried two combs. One for himself and one for the entire school building. Although by second grade most students came to learn of this two-comb system and fear of that one comb boys and girls would initiate combing their hair days before Mr. Foster's arrival. Yet still there was at least one occasion brought to my attention where a sweeping cootie epidemic broke out in the long history of Mr. Foster and his celebrated comb. At an age well before my time it was said the school was shut down for an entire two weeks as it waited for the school's nurse to give the clear from the school's cootie epidemic.

"No Neil," Mr. Foster began to explain. "That just won't do. You can use every ounce of saliva in that giant body of yours, but that hayfield on top of your head will become no less unacceptable. Now quit fussing and get up here!"

Reluctantly, Neil Finally approached our decorated photographer and after several firm swipes from Mr. Foster's questionable grooming implement Neil's hair was finally laid to rest.

"Okay class and again let's smile everyone and three two aannnn... relax. Well, I'm guessing this is just one of those days like Neil's bad hair. I don't believe I have ever had to stop for a second retake since my first year at this school. Neil that unkempt hayfield gave you two inches on Louis before I combed it down. Maybe in another year Neil, but for now you will need to switch places with Louis again. Sorry Neil."

I knew it! I just knew it. Sorry my ass. I knew I still stood superior amongst my classmates. Perhaps Moloch was right after all. Miss Frenchie and I are alike even if I was unable to see it yet, although somehow I had the feeling I soon would.

"Alright class let's try this again and together tightly close in once more," when at last I would nestle myself like a young offspring against his mother's colorful breast. Yes, as I imagined warm to the touch was she even if it was only one side of her flesh as her warm skin permeated itself throughout mine. Throughout my young body while a deluge of arousing stimulation went through me. Confirming all my feelings I had for her. Yes, her warmth I quickly clung to.

Only what came to suddenly pass I could not properly discern... While something beyond the warmth of another human being. Something more intensifying, more terrifying and evil. In my own disbelief I tried to pull away and from the energy to which now consumed her. Only this thing would not release me from her. This thing which now forsook my lover and I.

"And three, two, one. Smile everyone!"

Miss Frenchie suddenly reached out and squeezed her unforgiving hand onto my own. Then the emitting glow of the camera's shot surged into my eyes. Through this a streak of flashing bright light I instantly had a vision.

I saw the great Roman General Julius Caesar subdued by his fellow statesman who violently plunged their daggers into the up-and-coming usurper in an envious rage. After witnessing the last gasps of Caesar, another warmonger quickly invaded my already terrified vision. It was France's very own Napoleon Bonaparte whose many earlier victories now seemed distant and far from any one conquest. When next I viewed into the emperor's retreating Grand Army where Russia's cold grim winter released its dark shroud of death. From afar I could see the fierce burning flames of Moscow's glory while Napoleon himself dared to look back. Then as cruelly as the discharging lightning introduced itself, it just as swiftly withdrew.

"Perfect. A perfect shot children! Somehow, I believe this photo will become one of my best class pictures ever," I could hear Mr. Foster proudly proclaim while I staggered backwards against the wall behind me.

"Only what is this," I asked myself, "that has just befallen me? For what kind of love turns into this kind of evil so quickly and why has it found me? I am only a little boy who is only naturally curious about an emotion which enamors the soul. Besides, it came to me. Love came to me first. I never set out to look for her."

"The Snake, Moloch... It betrayed my first love. Turning it into a kind of evil. Luring me through its web of lies and deception. For it is in the Snake's habits to take away."

Only what kind of violent energy could surge throughout this seemingly beautiful creature as I first perceived? How could such energy exist? A force from nature with a capacity only the sun could duplicate.

Though why me? Why intrude my youth with these two war seeking mongers? For I have just begun to learn long division. Though still you pollute my mind with two demigods who sought to blot out the lives of so many. Pursuing in their desire to win their permanent fixture on all humanity.

"So I ask you Snake... why? Why me?"

"Louis. Louis!" Abruptly Mr. Foster would call out awakening me from my hypnotic state I found myself absorbed in.

"Better catch up with the rest of your class. Miss Frenchie will no doubt be waiting for you."

"Something Larger"

"Waiting for me!" I began telling myself over and over. Only why I continued with such senseless repetition I could not say. Though perhaps fear was my only answer. Fear which had taken hold of my being and my very soul as I found myself walking alone and inside an unusual silence along the school's long corridor. Anticipating an unknown which awaited me as I drew closer. Then without another thought or interruption in stride I quietly walked inside the classroom.

I immediately approached my desk and soon found myself staring from afar into a countenance I thought I knew. However, puzzled with an uncertainty while Miss Frenchie instructed the class with her usual relaxed composure. I felt as if now we were worlds apart. I waited for her to acknowledge me, to give me just one signal of warmth, but she continued our reading lesson without glancing in my direction at all.

"And remember class proper punctuation is critical as it directs the reader when to stop and begin a new sentence or it may ask you a question. A question which is pertinent to the reading at hand."

"Yes, the all-important question which simply is unavoidable," I now told myself with a rising confidence. It's what I will do. I will ask Miss Frenchie a most pertinent question. One not of insignificance, but one of accountability and to the point. It will sound something like this… "Who do you think you are? Luring me into your coercive unwelcoming love? Fitting only for your darkness with no possibilities for light to enter. While next asking, "Why me?

Why did I become your chosen one inside your ill game of depraved love? Was it simply due to chance or the fact I stood tallest amongst my class, hence placing myself next to you? For now I see that only darkness consumes your soul whereas any kind of light you forbid. We are nothing alike. Nothing!"

"No Louis."

"No Louis what? Whose voice now intrudes me. Moloch? What do you mean no Louis?"

"Are you not my friend Louis and as my friend are you not in need of my correction?"

"Your correction? Inside a labyrinth of only more corrupt corrections on my behalf? Only now leave. Go away. Go before I forsake us both!"

"Only what good would become of that? For it is only your stubbornness which betrays you and your lack of proper attention. You need only to pay attention Louis. Pay attention. For you and Miss Frenchie are everything alike. As she and others will remain your friend, I as well will remain yours. Only you must pay attention Louis. Pay attention!"

"And make certain children to wear your hat and gloves during recess or surely Mr. Steven will have each and every one of you back inside and sit with yours truly during your recess hour."

Unphased by the teacher's stark warning classmates all around me bolted from the classroom and toward another perilous recess hour leaving only myself behind. Myself with her along some uncertain script to be spoken between us.

For inside this carefree interlude I wasn't going to be pegged by some oversized red ball. This hour she was going to reveal and satisfy all her dark revelations. In other words, Miss Frenchie was going to give it to me straight! In moments I will walk up to her desk with purpose and an understanding she will know. Yes, that is what I will do!

Only now something peculiar suddenly occurred between me and the chair I now sat upon as the chair below me refused to release itself from me. For I tried though could not break from the strength it now held beneath me. When next I began to panic inside, wanting only to run away from the arena I now found myself inside. Yes run. Run Far away! Far away from she. Only now any occurrence to rise to my own two feet I found impossible.

Can she not see beyond the stack of assignments awaiting her? For now I sit alone. Alone inside a room of fear whose influence draws from a malign source. For why does she not speak? Speak plainly to me. Something. Say something to me, anything or just perhaps I will go mad!

Within the hours minutes slowly moving before us I began to wonder if Miss Frenchie would ever notice me again. Half an hour passed as I remained helplessly glued to my chair. Unmoved! Though perhaps my mouth, tongue and larynx would remain true and deliver the phonetic sounds and syllables used to form words. Then Miss Frenchie would have no excuse. She would feel compelled to answer my inquiries. My demands. From a love to which only seemed so certain only to be betrayed by its strange violence. Yielding no understanding, no mercies, no love. So I tried... I tried and I tried from where only silence grew. Where through its dark ambience controlled the fear inside me. Fear conveyed from within me. Then Miss Frenchie stopped!

Ceasing suddenly at last from the meaningless assignments before her Miss Frenchie slowly looked up. Drawing her gaze now solely in my direction with all her attention. Her countenance drawing closer as she motioned her one hand to come to her. The chair beneath me instantly releasing itself from below. At once finding myself walking toward her.

Miss Frenchie who I now stood before, gestured to the chair beside her. Obeying I willingly sat down. Immediately sending a chilling calm over me when next we surrendered our eyes to one another. She gave me her hand and from it all its immortal terror that had previously surged through me. A pervading silence surrounding us until her lips began to move.

"You have the gift Louis. The gift you hold inside you. A gift of great powers as I have myself."

"A gift? What gift do you possess teacher which lives also inside me?"

"Why it sits right before you and was formed inside the womb that nurtures you. Do you still not know this gift? Do you not remember me?"

"The Voice! Yes teacher, now I remember. Her lingering soft touch along her lips that satisfy my own. Unlike the known chaotic disruption and confusion of the Snake. Yes, she...? Is this the grandiose gift possessing me now?"

"No Louis. No! Not that wet fucking dream I have been giving you since your peculiar young lust began. For you confuse me with one who is me. The Snake Louis. Moloch is your gift. Without it the dream is without. She is removed. Can you not see, or do you see only with your eyes?"

"I can clearly see. It is you who is blind! Unlike you she holds no treachery over me as your disloyalty holds against me."

"You mustn't think so much Louis. Even to think I could bring harm to you. I am your friend who enables you, guiding you along life's uneasy path. This gift Louis is unequal, unparallel. Where few men possess but many envy. A gift Napoleon held as Julius Caesar drew upon as well. Only do you still not understand? Why I am here? Aiding you with something more?"

"Something More?"

"The crown Louis. The crown of the laurel wreath extending her strength with victory for those who want it. The gift Louis. The gift!"

"Strength and victory from a crown of foliage? What lies do you want me to believe now?"

"My beloved Louis, would I seek to harm you with lies? For only the immortals crown themselves with the laurel wreath."

"As Napoleon-Caesar himself?"

"Yes Louis as Napoleon-Caesar. Yes, now you begin to see. See from outside the comfort of your own eyes."

"Then I want to learn more about this foliaged crown and her strength she brings with her. Where can one find such a prized jewel?"

"To those before who have conquered the golden wreath." She spoke into my eyes. *"To the likes of Napoleon Caesar who now extend their immortal crown to those few who want and will accept her. For its magnitude reaches to the four corners of the earth of great Kings and emperors. While your journey began and continues with the Snake you yourself will achieve such splendors as the laurel wreath allows and like Napoleon-Caesar the crowned wreath will give you strength along the way."*

"Now let me ask you Louis, do you want her? Do you desire her powers and the victories she brings with her? Do you want to forever stand side by side great Kings and emperors...Napoleon-Caesar?"

"Yes, in all her perfection and entirety. Yes! For if what you say this crown and her strength creates this genuine living power only few men can attain then yes this is what I want. To stand in bronze amongst Kings and sovereigns where mere men only wonder. Only dream. Yes! Only I must ask why you have presented these great men who live inside their mortal ruins?"

"Why not the brave Gallic wars of Caesar or Napoleons absolute victories!"

"These triumphs the laurel wreath will grant you Louis, however with every greatness their comes a fall which few will elude. The fall will be great Louis as great as your celebrated rise."

"Then why? Why on the whole of God's green earth would I want to possess such a force to only fall violently into its path?"

"Have you not been listening Louis or do close your ears in jest when your teacher speaks to you?"

"No Teacher. I just want to understand more clearly, for after all I am only a child!"

"Then consider the magnitude of its scale Louis. More powerful than any tremble below the earth's surface. You cannot ignore this sovereignty when it is offered to so few. What could compare to a gift that can exceed in such glory and time filled honor? Nothing Louis. Nothing, except of course your own downfall, but you will have already achieved what mere mortals can only try to conceive in their limited imaginations."

"Well, could I think about it first? At least for this next coming night teacher. For this thing is much too great to just hastily hand over an answer in this passing moment."

"Think about it? Think about what Louis? What is there to think about? Was not Napoleon-Caesar feared at the very mention of their names and what about you Louis? Do the people fear you or do you fear the people? Did Alexander the Great think about conquering the Known world? The only thoughts which passed through Alexander was how will I conquer it! This you do not think about. This you want to immediately grab and seize onto. You do want to take hold of this laurel wreath don't you Louis or would you rather yield to the people who would chop off your head at the guillotine? Now you must take this laurel wreath and the downfall which follows or take nothing at all. That is it Louis for there is no thinking about!"

"Then I will choose. I will choose the only legitimate answer a mature man would submit to. I will choose the laurel wreath with all its glory. I will choose the crown of gold as Napoleon Caesar before me. I will choose my fate as well, however celebrated or desolate its end may come to pass. I will choose my immortality!"

"Good Louis. Wisely you have chosen, Chosen a passage which will allow you the strength few men have ever possessed while bestowing upon you an undeniable presence among your masses. You will be remembered among men, women & children."

"But the fall? What about the great fall teacher? How will this come to pass? Will my very peers willingly become my own murderous perpetrators, or will my final days be lived out on some distant island that is lost to the world amidst some vast ocean?"

"You will fall harder than most men, but you will always be remembered. This is all you need to know. With your great rise an even greater fall will follow. Sealing your destiny forever."

When suddenly her eyes grew more distant and with a waning, energy surging from me I started to cry out, "No teacher. Do not go! For you have not answered me as of yet. How will I fall? How will my final days fair with other men? Teacher... teacher, do not leave!

Leave me all alone with only that vile creature to accompany my every thought, every desire. Teacher wait! Only what now have I done? Dear heavens above what destructive fate have I so blindly yielded to? For I am only a man. Nothing more. Right? Though what if... what if I am something more? More than mere man. Something larger. Praised among men. Praised amongst the stars."

Then suddenly inside the likes of a whirlwind our transit eyes unlocked while her authoritarian hold released itself from me. At once finding myself alone sitting at my desk once again. When next slowly I looked up soon to observe the teacher resuming her earlier task. Grading our class assignments.

"When the Blood Drips"

With the end of third grade I was introduced to the beginning of another and although Miss Frenchie stayed true to her first and only husband she would never really leave me as the dream and her voice continued to grow inside me.

Now Miss Onassis guided me through the fourth grade then Miss Johnson through the fifth and so on and so forth. With each new teacher conveying her own esoteric voice through me. Thus maintaining the presence of the crowned laurel wreath I so now sought after.

In addition, a common element among each of these rare and unique instructors were their distinct loyalties to their proud ancestral pasts.

Miss Butahn from my sixth grade ardently claimed her family lineage to the thirteenth century Mongolian emperor Genghis Khan. It was said that for eight hundred years her family had secured proper evidence from this imperial ancestral line inside the distant vast Gobi Desert region.

Traveling further back in time my one eighth grade teacher Miss Constantine swore her family allegiance to a thousand year old empire dating back to 800 AD. Created by Carolus Magnus Charlemagne, the Holy Roman Empire endured until the coronation of another not so long ago emperor who decided this medieval empire was no longer needed. This emperor's name was Napoleon Bonaparte.

My tenth grade teacher and of a more recent age maintains her valiant family line from the heroic strength of one British general and statesman Arthur Wellesley. However, known more extensively from his title alone: 'The Duke of Wellington'.

These rarities acquired within my teacher's extraordinary ancestral personages in turn granted me the reassurance with each passing year that only a glorious future awaited me and that the laurel wreath continued to strengthen inside me. Truly I was now convinced of conquering and ruling a people one day, in order to offer them a proper government while deciding upon them their own subjected fate.

Only I asked the Voice, "When will this great ascent begin? What time in history will such glory arise? Tomorrow or just maybe next week or perhaps yet another, anxious long year? When will these distinguished gifts unfold? You have guided me throughout my youth and have given me correct counsel in all things and now I am almost a man. When Voice? When do such designed beginnings present themselves with their celebrated debut?"

"When the blood drips, Louis. You will rise when the blood drips from your own hands. You will ascend to the highest summit but the blood that drips must come first. Then you will soar to the sun Louis. You will soar with the likes of Icarus."

"But Voice, I said hastily, did not Icarus fly too close to the sun and perish?"

"Why yes Louis, Icarus did fly too close to the sun and plunged from the heavens. However, without his fall the greater ascension would have never taken place."

"And this blood you speak of? Whose blood will drip from my hands? For now I am beginning to believe the Snake has infiltrated your thoughts, hence yielding your mind to the methods of its perversion."

"Dummy! I am the Voice. When you seek out it you seek after me. For the ways of the Voice are the ways of the Snake. The ways of Moloch!"

"You lie! The Voice has always nurtured me as her very own, but never you!"

"How could I have chosen someone like you and now to waste all my prudent instruction with the likes of you!"

"Then why?" I pleaded. "Why did you choose me?"

"Because I love you Louis. Isn't that clear to you?"

"Love. Do you know the meaning? From my very existence you have only shown how malice and disorder work themselves together. Now leave me. Leave me now!"

"This Louis I cannot do!"

"Yes, I know. Oh, how I know from the deepest core of my being."

"Then will you drop this senseless parade of yours. For I love you and isn't that enough?"

"Perhaps and perhaps one day I shall love you as well… Only now I want to consider this blood you speak of. Whose blood? Whose blood will drip from my own hands and why must it come about?"

"Whose blood Louis? Why? Are you not able to meet your destiny head on? Did not Alexander the Great sacrifice thousands of people to those who tried to impede on his path? Did Julius Caesar not attach newly vanquished barbarian territories to add to the Romans' growing prestige with the slaughter of thousands and what about Napoleon? Do you truly believe that an emperor would cease mass annihilation if it stood in the way of victory? Why Louis? Why indeed."

"Forgive me. My own mindless recklessness. For I have yet to reach manhood though still I will not disappoint. Any servitude I bring will be of the highest order. You shall not regret the allegiance I pledge alongside my obedience to you."

"Good Louis. Your understanding at last emerges. With the perfection of the laurel wreath's strength firmly established inside you then will the blood begin to drip from your hands. Will your mission on earth reach its realization. Only you must wait Louis. Wait in long suffering. For the glory you embody requires patience. It will seek you out. It will pursue and guide you. Reward you in time."

"Miss Tolemy"

My senior year in high school had at last arrived and with its coming I legally became a man. I turned eighteen during my final summer school break and with this final departing year the last of anything ever to be handed over to me without a price. This would also conclude any formal instruction my youth with which could be forced upon me. The last of coerced decisions on my behalf as to what and how my education should be comprised.

This would also conclude any and all obstinate ideals that certain words need to be placed in some proper order to maintain their polite pose or the tactics of one whose instruction it was to convey some political agenda or, the has-been athlete whose only secured degree lies in physical education. Hence, I was properly in tuned to the distortion this schooling tried to govern as the Voice continued its guidance through this mire of more folly and opposition.

However, with every new school year one noteworthy teacher would always claim exception and this would be no different entering my final year of high school. Her name was Miss Cleo Tolemy and although she instructed proper English as another before her the words which emitted from her lips were imbued with a kind of romance others could not entertain. For Miss Tolemy was on that short list where her womanly qualities were presented in their purest forms. With her bold appearance outlining her soft ebony skin complimenting her silky black hair only a queen could wear. While her radiant blue eyes praised her petite countenance from which her pouting lips whispered through every breath she spoke. From her slender swanlike neck following downward toward further flawlessness and beauty.

Only these fleshly perfections alone could not have exposed the overall virtue of her existence. For not only had she never entered wedlock, but no man had ever entered her as well. At twenty-nine she still preserved her bodily excellence and with a chastity only an untouched woman could possess. Furthermore, Miss Tolemy also had an intriguing quality that set her apart from other teachers.

For the Voice always led me to those teachers who were in possession of some monarchal bloodline, or aristocratical past to which Miss Tolemy however would claim no such wealth. Now just maybe she was ignorant to any such grandiose claims, or just maybe she concealed any such royal rights to herself. Another likelihood, though one to which would sever this paradigm of teacher birthrights completely, would have to include the distinct possibility of her family never to have owned such privileges. Perhaps a long line of meager destitution followed her family's descent, however long or short that may be or just maybe she didn't care one way or the other.

In any case the absence of any true monarchal bloodline or any man ever lying down with her only proved to me how truly Miss Tolemy was going to be a very special match and for me alone.

Yes, clearly I could see this new creature before me who would inevitably become my first and absolute devotion towards a true and undivided love. For the others before her were a mere delusion of love while Miss Tolemy's love will sustain itself completely through its visible touch. Our love will speak to each other and glorify one another. Our love's prowess will dismiss all hate and rid all dark avenues and misfortunes.

Though most importantly our love will have the ability to destroy the Snake whose repeated malevolent behavior will at last succumb to the obedience of the Voice. The Voice of reason and compassion who instructs only untainted intentions and whose designs never pollute mankind. For the Snake is only a continuing germ of its own diabolical product crawling from beneath while praying for its next victim.

Thus, I waited. Waited anxiously anticipating the reappearance from the Voice. For the Voice had not spoken to me since the pre-arrival of my senior class. While days passed by then weeks when I began to yearn in restless wait for its next coming.

"The Assignment"

"Alright class please sit down and let's get started," Miss Tolemy patiently instructed her class. "I am very pleased with the hard work and effort you have all shown during these first few weeks on classical literature. Now for your many efforts I have come up with a very special class assignment to be based on a well-known and influential person of your choosing. This essay does not need to include centuries old material, although it will be welcomed if that's the direction you take. You might select an American president who has been influential or you might focus your attention on another leading political figure, whether here in the United States or in another country. The male or female figure of your choosing may reign under some higher government, or perhaps their leadership has contributed to humanitarian rights and the welfare of their own people or those abroad. Anyone or anywhere as the person and the story behind them will be entirely up to you."

"There will be three prerequisites required for this essay so listen up. First, proper grammar and punctuation always applies and second your essay should at least be 500 words to 1000 max. Now the last item is no less important so again, please listen carefully. As all of you should already know the historical facts in any given composition should always be your goal. Now with that said, I also urge you to choose that one individual who will speak to you in an intimate and personal manner. One whose ability has guided you or who could guide you forward each day. Someone you could follow to attain those personal goals and accomplishments."

"*Yes Louis, I am speaking to you. Pay close attention. Attention to your assignment containing that which you seek. The laurel wreath is what you long for. The crown that Napoleon-Caesar holds over you. The personal accomplishment that pursues you as you pursue it. Your destiny that will grant you glory. Your gift Louis predetermined by those who watch over you.*"

"Voice? Is that you? You who has come back to me? Come back and not forsaken me. Why it is you. Isn't it? I'm glad."

"*Yes Louis. It is I. Who would never leave nor forsake you. For I am not the betrayer's knife who offers no mercy upon the body of Caesar. No, I will sanctify you as Napoleon-Caesar You will shine within that same galaxy of stars. Even amid some forgotten island Napoleon was not forsaken. His name still lives. Survives on the tongue of so many. With fear does his name dwell, though with great compassion for those who seek out her laws.*"

"*One only needs to look back at the Roman Empire which had never truly fallen. For does not one continue to observe its pompous gallantry held high on marble pedestals amongst centuries of old ruins? While modern cities still look toward the empire for their own political and aesthetic advantages. Look to the laurel wreath which will become your personal pursuit. Your assignment carrying you to your destiny.*"

I continued to listen carefully to the teacher's steadfast parade of instructions. Only to soon find myself once again fused to the chair below me as her lips moved without pause. Observing now the empty desks around me. Unsure of it all. Could in fact the Snake now hold me against my will yet again?

This scene to reenact itself once more? I Knew that Miss Tolemy was different from the rest without pretentious blood lines looming over her. While no man has ever touched her flesh. Her soul. Only there it was rearing its ugly head at me once more. Why? Why does it enjoy this tasteless game. It now plays with me? To hold me against my own will and under its complete dominion. Where I asked? Where are you now Voice? Where are you who seeks not my submission but instead my continued loyalty alongside you?

"I am here Louis. I am always here with you. We are always here. For we are the same Louis growing only more steadfast for one another."

"Louis... Louis! You will be late for your next class Louis!"

"Yes Miss Tolemy," I had at last answered back. "I will be late for my next class."

Our eyes still locked, I knew I could have fallen into another trance, but quickly snapped out of her spell and hurriedly I left the classroom. I left her.

"She Will Speak to Me"

The following two weeks quickly passed as I was only all too consumed with my lofty new project which now I set out to breathe life into.

"Surely," I said to myself Miss Tolemy will be overcome with intrigue and reverence once she examines my essay subject and title which I will lay before her. What other collective name other than Napoleon and Caesar could such meaning and purpose be attributed to?

She will fall into my own illumination: A resounding light, mirroring the insight of spacious cities, entire nations, the Earth itself. She will see who I really am and observe the Caesarism and Napoleonic truths herself. A truth which will bring us closer and lead us down our magnetic path. When at last that day would arrive. Handing my essay Over to Miss Tolemy. Anxiously waiting next for the teacher's perfect mark. A mark to set me further apart from my fellow classmates. Then will she give witness to the only man sitting in the room. A man who resembles not a mere boy, but one who is capable of understanding a woman's touch.

Only now the days that followed somehow slowly went by as I waited for her long-awaited praise. A glorified adulation only men are capable to receive. When finally that day would come unannounced from inside the remaining minutes of class as she began to methodically hand over our prized assignments one essay at a time:

"Good job Sara!"

"Fine work Karl."

"A little more research Theodore and certainly you will receive an 'A' next time." Came the approvals from Miss Tolemy.

Only what praise will she hand me? Will she anoint my name before the class and deliver her love to me and me alone? When soon my would-be lover would appear over me.

Only now I asked myself, "What is this? This dramatic theatrics to which now stares over me?"

For now she glares over me from a silent pause before handing my essay back to me. Only something was not right. Something was wrong! Moloch. As I now read her mark and from my very eyes seemed to betray me. Finding myself turning the title page at every possible angle. However, the despairing reality becoming quite clear and immediate-FAILURE! A crystal clear 'F' that all at once defeated all hope. For now our love to only come crashing down before it could even create itself a beginning.

Though perhaps through my excitement my language failed to manifest itself through the material I so selectively chose? For now I sat and pondered. Unsure. However, I knew the Voice to give only clear thoughts, order and meaning through the words I chose. Does not misunderstand the error in her ways, but the Snake does and is predisposed in its errors. Moloch must have infiltrated itself inside the text of these pages. Disguising itself deceptively while securing my trust then coercing my mind to hand then from pen to paper only to end in blatant error.

"Louis...Louis Ney! Helloooo...I'm speaking to you."

"Yes, Miss Tolemy? I suddenly responded from my thoughts spinning out of control.

"Yes Miss Tolemy. Yes of course!"

"Good. We will talk after class, she said then continued to hand out further praises.

Yes, I told myself. We will talk after class. Speak to one another. However, in view of the situation before me I did not feel the discouragement or dismay one might think. No, for Miss Tolemy and I will soon speak to one another and then will I begin to explain myself and make her understand. Understand our love for each other cannot exist on a failure. It can only flourish and thrive within an untainted state of perfection. I will make her see that our love can only survive if void of any and all discrepancies. "Good job overall on those essays class. Keep up the good work and I will see you all back here tomorrow. When the last student left the classroom she turned to me, Louis we only have a few minutes before my next class, so please bring your chair up to my desk along with your essay."

"Louis? Louis do you hear me? Louis! Why is it you stare at me so? Louis bring your chair up here now!"

"Louis, she's waiting for you. Get up Louis. Go to your teacher."

"Now Louis!" Miss Tolemy called out.

"Yes teacher, I am coming." I began to speak from within. In order to make an account for myself. My abilities in which you have clearly overlooked. I am coming though will seek no prejudice as our love is stronger than any single trifle misconception you may have errored in. "Please sit down Louis," and soon found myself from across her desk and caught up in her gaze while her maternal instruction began to speak to me. "Now as your teacher Louis I will be as straightforward with you as I can. So please do not view any of my next remarks mean or dispirited in nature. With that said I am not sure what you were striving for here, but this composition you turned in was much to do about nothing. A lot of idle words here Louis and this Napoleon-Caesar you fused together it seems more imaginary than anything else."

"Imaginary Miss Tolemy?" I asked trying to decipher the words which now came off her lips. Only now what am I to believe? An instruction controlled by dogma and mere make believe?

"Why yes Louis. You left the reader with very little facts and lacked any real coherency. A lot of fanciful suggestions and this laurel wreath maintained over and over again alongside its strengths. What strengths Louis and why is this laurel wreath so important? These things you should have explained to your reader. The mood of your essay just doesn't convey any clear and specific theme other than more of the same continued gibberish. While this dripping blood from the hands of Napoleon-Caesar as you put it. What is it you are trying to express here? I'm sorry Louis, but you seem to have missed the entire assignment as to the meaning of how these men influenced you now or in some past. What is this Louis? What is the meaning of this wreath and this dripping blood you find so intriguing? Meaningful?"

"Answer her Louis. Answer your teacher!"

"You can speak now. I would also like to hear your thoughts. Louis...Louis."

"Because the blood does drip! Continually forever from their hands Miss Tolemy. I spoke from within its sudden instruction from the germ to which dwells inside me. Moloch. For the wreath's strength and vitality can only emerge from the blood that drips. An influence these two men offer to mankind. A collective vision in their response toward defeat of the weak."

"Hmmm," Miss Tolemy reflected momentarily. "Though perhaps you could have utilized more material from the many military and political achievements or lack of from these two men."

"Lack of? You speak now from a woman's lips. For any 'lack of' only proves irrelevant in comparison to the longevity these crowned heads bestow upon posterity and beyond."

"In any case Louis, I believe your assignment has lost any real meaning." Her eyes now stared widely back at Unblinking. "Out of touch with any true reality and while I should also think this dripping blood is more than a little inappropriate for this assignment. Don't you think? Simply referring to this dripping blood would have been more than enough?"

"She now speaks without govern Louis. Neither bridle to hold back her treacherous tongue. Therefore Louis, correct her error and speak through me now."

Hence, I began to speak from the words of Moloch and through her prolonged stare over me.

"Though what is reality Miss Tolemy when the truth suddenly behaves inappropriately? For the blood to which drips from their hands, drips perpetually. While the pen alongside its sword sweeps away, thousands of lives inside moments of time. Napoleon-Caesar is no illusion. Their time on earth no mistake. For there is nothing inappropriate when men as such maintain loyal diligence in the minds of so many. While generals envy their names, they comparatively justify their own means to their own end. Even mere citizens, reach out in their futile attempt to lure the seductive pomp it awards these men."

When next I would await her reply while reflecting on those truths and how they would infuse her with fear. I knew the strange mannerisms of the Snake and how it used me as a vessel to deliver its evil.

Only still I carefully mused over the polite pose she still carried before me, Perhaps she has come to understand? Who I am and would become? Then she would stand by me. An autocratic reincarnate of Napoleon and Caesar. An entity now seated before her very eyes as I now sat quietly waiting for her lips to speak to me again. While from a strange silence filled the ambience of the room, its relentless rant continued to inundate itself inside me. Moloch, laying siege to the very thoughts of my reasoning. Thoughts of who or what is genuine or not.

When at last Miss Tolemy would interrupt those thoughts.

"You have made several good points here Louis," came the unexpected though welcomed approval from her lips. Perhaps we could discuss this subject further. Though at a later time. After school? Here in my classroom? We will talk more on this subject you find so fascinating. You are fascinating Louis... aren't you? After school Louis. I will be waiting."

I knew she would understand, I told myself as I left the classroom. With a euphoric pleasure to which comes along with the anticipation from your first genuine love. For now I knew the others were in fact a mere delusion of my imagination. While to now understand my love, our love could only be that of an extension of the laurel wreath itself.

A love you know will happen. Will come into existence. Though you have no idea for how long it will survive. A year, perhaps weeks or even a year long or just maybe forever but you know it will arrive. It will come to you and that is the only thing that matters as you impatiently wait for her to come to you.

My final two classes slowly crept along with my thoughts centered on her. My teacher. My Miss Tolemy, as I waited anxiously for that last tolling bell to conclude another day. My strides were long and steadfast when the bell finally summoned me to her.

"I knew you would come to her Louis. To me. For I have given her to you, but only this once will she come into you. You belong to me Louis. Now speak to her as she sits before you."

"Here I am Miss Tolemy. Can you see me? I am here!"

"I can see you!" She slowly spoke as she raised her head from the current assignments she was marking. "For you stand before me now. Though please sit down."

Immediately I sat on the chair I had left across her desk earlier, while she picked up my essay she had set aside from the stack of papers around her.

"Here it is. Your essay we spoke of earlier. Yes, this fascinating laurel wreath which holds all this power for you. Yes, fascinating indeed."

"Only what fascinates you right now Louis? This entwined crown of branches and leaves or this warm flesh that awaits you? Sits before you?"

"Yes, Miss Tolemy. Yes!"

"Yes what Miss Tolemy?" Her demand promptly snapped back at me.

"The wreath Miss Tolemy and the reward along with it."

"Then we should not think twice entertaining one another in a more relaxed setting. My home is near Louis. Ten ten Lotus Way."

"She is a Woman After All"

"Ten ten Lotus Way," I repeated aloud as I counted down until I reached my destination.

"1042…,1034…,1014…,1012…,1010!" My eyes immediately fixated on the letterbox of my lover's dwelling. The numerical address alone delivering chills inside my covetous flesh. For I knew inside was she. She who would announce herself to me. Her love for me.

When first I observed my lover's domain I understood how unique she was and how strikingly attractive from the ordinary homes around her. For the others lined the street with only more of the same tedious ranch styled homes or the other kind of two story dwellings which drew only upon their own simplicities. Miss Tolemy's however wore a sophistication with an imposing splendor the others could not compare.

Standing amongst a narrow grove of tall white birch a large two story reddish brown brick home maintained its humble though dignified appearance. Through its miniature monarch like ambience, ornate white pillars stood boldly with their own Corinthian capitals. An oversized door also stood between the two pillars as it was glazed with a fine dark varnish and directly above the door hung a square balcony enclosed with a black wrought iron railing. Flanking the balcony were two neatly trimmed white dormers each with its own wood shutters. A small, gilded dome which crowned the rooftop was adorned with a handcrafted lady of victory. She stood proudly on a golden crest overlooking the home's majestic landscape.

'Yes,' I told myself. For what other prize could be handed down to me with such bounty?

When soon a lone red cardinal quickly stole my attention away as I watched it fly inside the small grove of white birch. Landing from one branch to another until at last satisfying itself on one taller branch. While always carefully observing the surroundings around her when again my attention was at once swept from under me. For at last my lover would appear unannounced. Perched on the balcony's black iron platform as if to mimic the red cardinal nearby. While her translucent white robe hugged decadently near her body, her dark silky hair blew gently with the wind. In awe of her rich, bold beauty and ebony skin she quietly beckoned me to come inside.

Now I knew she would be mine. Understood from those delicate behaviors, as now my compliancy drew my steps closer to her. Pausing briefly before the first three steps the porch would lead me. A passage staring back at me when soon I would slowly open the door.

Once inside I found myself in a rather spacious foyer with an ocean blue backdrop covering the walls. To my immediate left a dark walnut staircase presented itself and from its summit I surmised, would my lover soon come down. At the bottom of the staircase near one corner stood a tall mahogany coat rack with a lone white wool coat hanging from it and where I now hung my own coat. A plain wood bench also sat near the door of the foyer though its plainness appeared offset by the colorful array of fancy footwear lined around it. Next I turned to the opposite side of the staircase where two large oil on canvases hung next to each other.

The first painting featured a young mother somewhere inside the nineteenth century. She donned a brilliant blue hooded cloak that set her apart from the drab landscape behind her. Close to her bosom lay a sleeping babe. Its mother was nothing more than a mere child herself and her expression revealed a sad wonderment of perhaps those inevitable struggles she would soon encounter herself one day or perhaps already has.

Hanging next to this painting, was one of a tall, albeit overly thin man dressed in a black suit and bow tie. The overall image was dark and the dim background looked somewhat eerie. The English fancied gentleman appeared weary and whose face was stricken with a sort of calamity, however soon to be relieved of both these humble subjects as I turned to the staircase summit once more.

"Hello Louis. I am glad you came. I have been waiting for you!"

Only now I could not move my lips to respond. My body standing motionless as well. For now her body proved more desiring than from any classroom hour as only my eyes seemed to move. While carefully observing her unhurried, graceful descent downward. The light from the landing window revealing the splendid outline of her nakedness through her airy white gown. Unveiling every secret to which I now understood. At last she stepped toward me. Her maternal love, coming closer until her budding rose nipples gently brushed against my chest. Leading me through a set of varnished French doors to a room. Obediently I followed.

At once I could see her appreciation for those finer things become even more evident. From the adorning soft yellow wallpaper with tiny white and violet petals accompanied by their forest green stems with still more stories on canvases scattering the four walls. Not surprisingly stood a tall bookshelf as I stayed close behind, quickly scanning through an assortment of titles displayed their bounded covered spines, Mary Shelley with her Frankenstein creation to Hawthorn and his subdued candid taboo inside the pages with Hester and her scarlet letter. Within reach of these literature geniuses an older unembellished rocking chair sat close by. Though most notably was the grand piano (at least a century old) placed center stage where my lover's taste for Chopin revealed itself.

Adhering closer still to my lover, I could see a sweeping view of the sun setting to our west through a set of large bay windows. Beneath a dark green plush deep, buttoned sofa that we soon found ourselves sitting on. Where now she sits near me. Her delicate features and blue eyes illuminated by the afternoon sun.

"You're staring at me Louis." She said, smiling. "Hasn't anyone ever told you it's impolite to stare?"

"Forgive me teacher. My good manners must have strayed from me momentarily. I replied though without any real attempt to divert my gaze at all."

"It was only in jest my dear," she said as she placed a gentle hand on my knee. "You have nothing to worry about. In fact I enjoy your eyes on me. But now I would like you to address me by my first name- Cleo."

"Cleo, I softly said, testing the word on my tongue."

"Did you like uttering my name? Does it please you Louis?" She asked.

"Do I please you Louis?" I who have given you everything and you who gives back only continued "betrayal."

"Louis, Louis I asked if I please you?!"

"Yes, yes you please me, of course. Most certainly Miss Tolemy. Uh, I mean Cleo."

How could you not please me? I thought before a sense of surrealism engulfed me. Another suddenly trying to take over me. Its voice commanding her lead. She was not the teacher I had known previously. There were no formal instructions to comply with in this setting as inside the classroom. No, something simpler passed through her now. A grace I had not witnessed prior. Lust had been freed from within her. Now, she aired her every movement and expression like a carefree performer on some stage.

"Louis! Louis, are you there? Can you hear me?"

"Yes... is that you Miss Tolemy?"

"It is I"

"Yes Miss Tolemy. I mean teacher... no, Cleo."

"Relax Louis. You needn't be afraid. For I am that gift. That comfort. That pleasure. Only now come with me. Follow me once more."

So I followed. Near her lead once again where from only a few steps away the dining room received us. Boasting only a minimal of furnishing the room however still held onto its Victorian charm. While more paintings scattered the soft pink walls, one large framed mirror hung above a buffet. A small round table with its four ornate chairs completed the room's modest appearance with a white cloth covering the table's surface as a table for two had already been set.

Immediately we sat and she reached for the bottle of red wine that awaited us. Silently she began to pour large amounts into each glass, then moved her seat closer to mine. Her breath whispering across my face.

"Drink Louis. Drink to us and to your Napoleon-Caesar." Her words asserted their loyalty to our deep union. So I drank. I drank From the glass placed before me and began to relax. My flesh, my mind uninhibited when she began to ask...

"Do you love her Louis? Do you love her the way you love me?"

"Do I love her?" I now asked myself confused by the unexpected scrutiny. For who am I capable to love? Who stirs my very imagination whose name alone is spoken? Who could I love more?

"Well Louis, do you? Do you love her?"

"Her?" I now reflected aloud. "Who is HER? And does this 'her' belong to me or perhaps another?"

"Do not be coy with me Louis. I see you both walking side by side in the hallways at school. Every day I watch her. I watch the both of you, but most of all I watch you."

"From the rising sun through its descent, I watch over you."

"Only now you need not watch over me. You need to go away. Go away!" I spoke from under my breath. "Leave me alone."

"Away Louis? I cannot do that. I am that gift. That tangible apparition. Go away...?"

"No teacher." I put my head down in bewilderment. "Not you whose blood runs through my own. For now these words were spoken for another."

"I see. Then please continue telling me about this girl who you seem to ardently deny any love for."

"Yes teacher, the girl, whose sudden remembrance quickly overcame my true focus sitting before me. For what interests could this serve? Though it now seemed she was jealous as I began to regretfully call upon the girl."

"This girl? I certainly do not love her! We are....we are friends, more or less."

"More or less? More or less what Louis? Less of friends and more of something else? What more is this you share with her? More than you share with me."

"Well, you know teacher. Things. We have done things."

"Things? What things?"

"We have done things, but not that."

"Then you have kissed her? You have tasted her lips with your own?"

"Well yes, we have done that. That much we have done."

"Only there is more." She gently implored. "Do you want to keep me guessing or will you be the man you are capable of being?"

"I have laid my head upon her and touched her flesh with my own!"

"How Louis? How have you touched her flesh and how have you laid your head upon her? How have you done these things?"

"I have laid my head against her chest!"

"Her maternal devotion!" she quipped. "I think you do love her."

"No!" I replied almost vehemently. "For she lives without any true maternal anatomy that could nurture me."

"And because of this you do not love her? Then I should think this time will be different. For I am not without that maternal gift which this girl seems to lack. No, this time will be different. You will lay your head on my bosom and you will taste my sweat as I comfort you wholly from inside my womb!"

"Yes Louis. This is from a creation I have given you. This womb you have known from our beginning."

"Now Louis, this girl. How have you touched her?"

"The girl?"

"Yes, the girl."

"I slid my two fingers inside her." At last I told all. "I have done that. I have experienced the pool of warmth from inside the flesh of a woman. The scent of her being. I have done that."

"So, you have not yet known her fully? You are yet to look completely inside her. You haven't fucked her Louis!"

"No, no teacher, I have not done that. We have not done that For only the tips of my fingers have known her that way."

"And still you do not love her. Why? After all doesn't she possess that one female quality true to any given woman regardless of her abilities to nurture or not?"

"I could never love her. Though you speak with some truth, I still could never love her!"

"Why can't you love her? Don't you want to love her?!"

"No teacher, never! Never could I love a creature like her. She is nothing like with your radiant skin. Admittedly, it is a peculiar attraction I don't quite understand. For her skin is so fair it is detesting to my eyes. Have you ever seen fairer skin? White as fresh snow covering the length of her body and those veins...those intricate green veins running like a map over her anorexic body. Her unpleasing flat chest unveils only more green lines where her capacity to nourish is lost. My eyes rested admiringly on my teacher's ample breasts. Only large buds protrude from that surface."

"And this is why you do not love her? Due to the skin given to her at birth? To me this is a very curious thing, though I welcome it at the same time. That is, your taste or lack of it with this girl from that of my own flesh you seem to revere so passionately. I would like you to tell me more about this girl's inferior flesh as you put it."

"But it's not just her skin that I find distasteful. Not only are her breasts inadequate, but her hips could never serve any true purpose. Those angular, anorexic hips would no doubt prove their deficiency for any normal childbearing. Besides, I came to understand that I could never love this girl once I studied her mother. Her husband deserted her long ago. Probably because she dons the same anorexic clothes as her daughter. Even now, her middle age hips still resist another inch as does her entire body. Now those nipples cannot be so tender anymore as and those bones branch through that flesh just a little bit more."

"Then why do I see you walking the halls everyday with this girl that you find so undesirable? Displeasing in your mind? Why?" "She is a woman after all," I blatantly spoke before sipping from my glass, "and this peculiar attraction is still nevertheless a noteworthy desire of sorts. Her image still possessing a practical means though I should think the greater explanation of her appeal lies from her youth which subdues any unacceptable traits. Her Flesh is firm and soft and has the aroma of a virgin."

"Then you have saved yourself Louis, like I have? For that special someone who is more worthy?"

"Yes, I spoke through a lust that only our eyes continued to transmit. I have saved myself teacher."

"Then this is a very honorable thing. Only be careful with whom you choose to love or not to love. Do not allow your flesh to take over and care more for that restless lover who resides inside us all. There are those who only want immediate gratification and they endure no real patience. Unleashing their untamable lust. Stay far from this kind of lover but keep near those who are able to manifest their steadfast patience. For they desire not just your carnal needs but whose true needs that surface when trouble arises. These people do not turn yourself from." She paused to gather her thoughts.

"What I am really trying to tell you is this - I am the only love you need to keep by your side. For my lust for you rivals any great lover, and my patience is like no other. Do you hear me, Louis?"

"Yes, I can hear you," I replied as I observed my teacher's prudence.

"More wine my lover?" She asked before I produced an empty glass.

"Again, you are staring at me. What do you see? Though it must please you immensely to be here with me."

"Yes teacher," came my slow and sole response, my words now drunk with wine.

"Yes teacher, what? What Louis? What is it?"

Though I was not sure what it was. But she now sat before me with an attraction that seemed like an apparition of facets that I could not entirely understand. Though at the same time I knew her appearance and her voice was one I had known.

"Do you think I am pretty? More pleasing to the eyes? Prettier than her?"

"Do I think you are pretty, teacher? More than her?"

"Yes Louis, but please do not do that. Do not repeat my words. Now I asked if you think I am pretty or do you loathe me like that whore you dip your fingers into, exploiting her solely for her youth?"

"Of course you are more pleasing to the eye teacher. How could I ever loathe a creation like yourself?"

"Though I wonder how Louis? How am I as pretty as you say I am?"

"As the sun never fades and whose subjects know no darkness...." My words began to Flow from an excitable passion. "From where cascades interrupt dark depths of vast forests. This is how teacher. How your light never leaves you. Your beauty is always present. Always near"

"Why you are a poet and a pleasant one at that. Though still I wonder? I wonder if you will lie down with me inside your green forests where your cascades flow or hold me where your sun never dies? I wonder about these things, Louis, but most of all I ask myself if you will come inside me, and search who I am? Explore you and I? This I want to Know."

"Yes teacher. Yes!" I called out. "Yes, I will explore you and I and receive your Flesh inside my own. Yes!"

"Oh, you want me. You want to fuck me! Tell me Louis. Tell me and don't hold back!"

"Yes, teacher, I want you. I need to touch and smell your virgin flesh, This I want. I desire and to taste the dew that drips off your body when the morning sun rises. To hold you and breathe into you. Yes, I want you."

"But is it me you really want or that albino slut who you refer to as an acquaintance? Tell me Louis. Say it... You want to fuck me! Say it Louis. Say it!"

"Yes, I do. I do!"

"Then tell me Louis. Tell me you want me! Let me hear those words come from your own lips!"

"I want to fuck you!" I suddenly cried out while at last understanding her desire to hear those words. "Yes teacher, Yes, I want to fuck your soft ebony skin. Your virgin path where none have entered. Yes Miss Tolemy, I want to fuck you!"

Pacified by the words she so fervently demanded from me, she began to rise slowly until her lustful eyes stared over me, commanding me to stand alongside her. I obeyed. My teacher. My Miss Tolemy whom I now stood next to and who I now understood. Understood its meaning…"Fuck me."

"Come my lover," she whispered her instruction to me. "Let us finish what we started in a more comfortable setting. My bedroom is upstairs," and once again I followed and we retraced our steps back to the foyer where the enigmatic eyes of the babe's mother, and the hapless gentleman in the paintings followed us.

Her lead was soft and gentle where my eyes now maintained their diligent pursuit of the loosely fitted gown that bounced ever so lightly against her perfectly round ass. When she mounted her final step, she immediately reached for my hand and would next usher me through a strange corridor. Though unlike the warm Victorian motif below. A corridor both unfinished and bleak. There were no stories told on canvases, just undecorated walls faded over time. The two bedrooms we passed were just as bare and unfinished and quite vacant as well until our passage would abruptly end.

When we reached her room it was if the room itself stared back at me. Deciding my worthiness to step inside her or not. But my desire to enter quickly diminished any self-doubt and at last she would welcome me inside.

Still hand and hand, I could at once feel the warm invitation from my lover's sanctuary. In stark contrast to the cold, vacant corridor, the wallpaper design looked fit for a palace. I had no doubt that the flamingo pink covering with its soft petals and leaves would have met Queen Marie Antoinette's approval. The trimmed ceiling with its gilded crown molding added to the room's monarchical ambience, as did more timeless paintings. A tall black oak dresser with a swivel mirror stood by the only window in the room and a nightstand beside the bed also had a black oak finish with a small lamp on it.

My eyes grew wide with anticipation as she led me toward her lavender linen bed. When I reached her alter, I Freed my obedient hand and looked hungrily into her eyes.

"I love you, Louis. I love you more than you will ever love me." More? I curiously wanted to know.

"How can you love me more than I could ever love you? For your ways are perfect and untainted. No, you can never love me as I love you."

"Never Louis? For I have always loved you more. While now you love this girl more. But this girl will forsake you as you have forsaken me."

"No, not true. Never will our love be forsaken. Never!"

"Do not speak another word to me Louis. For now I have grown weary from all your insolent delusions on my behalf. Now you need only to observe what I have given to you."

Hence, watching her I continued to listen to the Voice while standing before its commanding silence. Observing the stillness between us until her hands moved slowly up to her shoulders. Only briefly pausing before removing the loose-fitting garment which fell gently at her feet.

Our breaths were rampant without restraint as her naked body stood in restless pose. An image to which did not equal previously inside my mind. For her breasts nurtured a flawless oval appearance and firmness from where her rounded nipples peaked. While a well preserved stomach remained unblemished from any childbearing trauma as her hips remained untouched as well.

Before me, in all her glory, stood a sculptured black goddess whose luminous skin beckoned my own. With her approval I began to tear at the covering which hid my own naked flesh. At once our stares growing heavier alongside our breaths as our bodies now both stood naked before one another. A pulsating stimulant my body's inner energy could not properly explain, though one I could never tire from. When at last she stepped away from her gown and fell into my arms.

An immediate unbridled hunger now raged through our warm bodies as I firmly held her strong back and used my free hand to cup her curvaceous ass. Her head lying restlessly on my shoulders. Moving her hips against my own. A licentious excitement my body could not nor want to stop at this time. Two naked bodies pressing incessantly against each other as if today was all we had.

Tirelessly we held on to each other until my lover, Miss Tolemy, raised her head from my shoulder. She looked at me tenderly before her lips drew closer toward mine. An unthinkable passion I had not previously known. Unlike Miss Tolemy, the albino schoolgirl could only arouse me superficially. Miss Tolemy, however, was my true lover and at last touch my lips with her own. Her warm breath awakening my every sense until we unleashed an untamable hold through the probing of our wet tongues.

"Touch me Louis. Touch me!" She spoke, when next I pulled my hand away from her firm ass and slid my two fingers inside her. I could feel her moans and calls vibrating from within her. "Louis... Louis...." Her warmth was moist and her fragrance, which we now shared, was soft and erotic. I rubbed my other hand up her back and firmly gripped her head, pulling her lips still closer to mine. Only to just as quickly draw away from her wet kisses to enjoy her means of approval while I continued to govern my fingers inside her. "Fuck me, Louis, Fuck me!" she cried out.

"Fuck me!" And soon her body's pulsating rhythm throughout her hips guided my two fingers deeper inside my steadfast devotion.

"Yes, Louis. Yes, yes." she cried out until her body yielded to a series of euphoric, spasmodic jolts. Twitching without restraint her hips convulsed with a culmination of excitement.

"Yes! Yes, yes Louis…yes!"

When soon the two wet fingers I ruled inside her I pulled away. Allowing the euphoria of her lust to take its course. Reaching behind her firm ass once again, I now relaxed the strong hold of her head and listened to her quivering breaths. Our bodies bathed in one another's sweat. "Yes Louis, yes." Her only response continued and grew only more impatient with her incessant, lustful needs. When finally she gently pushed my own restless body down on the bed, enforcing her dominant will over me. The action was unexpected, but welcomed. For in those moments that followed, she would mount her own maternal body against my own.

Her mount was wet and warm when she firmly placed herself upon me as I allowed myself to yield to her chivalrous love. Stroking my long, wispy hair and smooth face with her impassioned touch. When soon she began to thrust her gentle dominance against my own hips as I took the invitation to gently strike back.

Her thrusting lips remained moist as she continued to strike her mounted lover. Pleasing herself once more and releasing her sweet aroma. Soon she would culminate her will once again, as she continued with unbound restraint. While now a momentum less frequent though more powerful than before. Slamming her wet pussy against my mounted ass as she continued her labor in growing satisfaction.

"Yes Louis. Come to me," she repeated each time she struck. "Come to me!" As she thrusted with more excitement than before as her trembling body paused longer from each previous assault.

"Yes teacher," I wailed in applause.

"Yes, my Miss Tolemy. Yes!"

When at last she released her final moans as I held on to her trembling ass and from the swelling ecstasy dripping from her. Her final climax at last celebrated as she turned toward me once more and began to kiss my lips once again.

"Untitled"

Our clandestine meetings would continue their weekly decadent appearances and from the strength through its Voice would summon me again and again.

Once a week Miss Tolemy would welcome me to her home from a never changing ritual of neither day nor time. An encounter of déjà vu I would hail upon each week. Gone were the stuffy suits and boring slacks my teacher would don each school day. Instead, when perched upon her modest balcony at 1010 Lotus Way, her sensuous white gown loosely hugged her sleek and sultry ebony skin. She always lured me inside and never once did our private arrangements deviate.

That lone red cardinal would never fail to appear just before my lover's unannounced appearance stole my attention. Once inside the foyer I would then be greeted by the subjects in the paintings: mother with child and the ill-fated Englishman. Then from the staircase, Miss Tolemy would suddenly emerge once more. Pausing briefly with the same licentious appeal I had come to know so well. Always gently brushing against me just before we passed through the French doors to the formal sitting room. A place where her warmth would materialize as she led me to that plush green sofa one more time. Where I would envision her pouting lips touching mine as I looked into her deep blue eyes. Then I would yield to her every maternal arousal, ready to take to her protruding rosebuds offered beneath her silky white lingerie. However, just like every other time I would soon follow her too the dining room and settle at a table set for two. Where we always enjoyed sharing a bottle of red wine which coerced my lips with confession.

For nothing deviated. Drifted from its natural course. In her bedroom always she placed her lover softly down on her bed before mounting my body and carrying out her maternal act. She cradled my needs, held me in her arms while commanding her flesh deeper into my own. Seeking a climax we both had never known. While always faithful and loyal she would come into me. Come into us. But then something changed our ritual and the words she spoke betraying the only love that mattered. A love that was genuinely pure and uncalculated. A love that didn't conform to the restrictions of man's laws. This love, or so I thought, was boundless and from an Eden unexplored.

"Please Do Not Go!"

"L ouis."

"Yes Miss Tolemy, Here I am. Here I am always."

This day always came without exception. Her pretentious words once again supported by the illusionary notion that my school work was somehow lacking and not within the limits of a certain standard. On the contrary, I knew the material I presented was unblemished. The reality was that Napoleon-Caesar always drew us together and the strength of our union would continue to lure me to 1010 Lotus Way.

"I would like a word with you after class."

"Certainly Miss Tolemy," came the words I had grown accustomed to saying.

"Good, I will see you then," she concluded before turning her attention back to the class. "Good job on those essays. Keep up the good work and I will see you all back here tomorrow!" With those forever departing words I would once again find myself at her desk.

"Alright then Louis I'll come quickly to the point and tell you why I want to speak with you," she would begin as I acknowledged her sovereign lips across from me once more.

"Firstly, you performed well at the start of this school year, however, your grades do not reflect these achievements in the second semester.

In fact, you are barely getting by. Is everything alright at home? How are you getting on with your other classes and classmates?"

"Everything is fine Miss Tolemy. I am fine. We are fine." Though soon would grow disturbed from her initial questioning. For always she opened with her displeasure for Napoleon-Caesar, albeit through her own erroneous thinking. Only now she asks of any discomfort I may have incurred from home or from other classmates. While now she seems to speak to another. An individual not of myself rather one whose weekly habits differ from that of my own. Though still I would continue to anticipate her eventual correction of events we always followed week after week.

"That's good Louis. I'm pleased to hear that everything is alright, but now I would like to discuss one particular assignment. The one that involved a historical figure of your choosing and whose influence seems to have certainly reached you. Do you remember this?"

"Certainly I do Miss Tolemy. I replied." I remember it from its infancy.

"From its infancy Louis?"

"Yes, from its birth it was and became."

"Became…" She paused momentarily. "At any rate, you chose these two great men in your essay. Caesar and Napoleon."

"Yes, Miss Tolemy. Napoleon-Caesar."

As I would remain ever so perplexed by her uncertainty, but I was also relieved when the combined names, Napoleon-Caesar, exited her lips. As always, this name became more unified with each passing week. In turn this united us.

When next I anxiously asked, do you now find Favor within the name, "Napoleon-Caesar?" Hoping the mere mention of "Napoleon-Caesar" would act as a Key to her heart and procure an invitation to 1010 Lotus Way. I knew it was only a matter of time before she surrendered to its name I so ardently spoke upon.

"Yes Louis, okay, I like the way you have merged these two names. But asking me if I favor their name? I suppose it is not so clear what you mean…" Her voice trailed off and faded strangely from me.

"Why yes, Miss Tolemy, that is why we are here is it not? Louis, I asked you to stay back to discuss your unfortunate decline in grades since that essay assignment."

"A decline in grades?" I uttered quietly back. Where now her lips spoke from an enigmatic dialogue from which 1010 Lotus Way eludes her memory. For the essay along with its subject, Napoleon-Caesar unites our meetings. Not any decline in grades thereafter.

Hence, I implored further. "The paper Miss Tolemy. The essay and its failing mark. That is why we are here. The essay!"

"Well, yes Louis but also I can tell you that your decline in grades since have remained steady throughout this semester. You were an 'A' student. Am I making any sense here Louis? Can you see the point I am trying to make?"

"No, you cannot see Louis. For you see nothing without me. You and this bitch who blinds your sight from me. I told you to only love us. What we have is certain, unlike what you claim to have with this bitch that you appeal to every week. Greed has overtaken you. It has taken you from me. You leave me no choice, Louis. Now I shall seek out to terminate this invented love from you!"

"No. Leave her alone!" I demanded addressing the interloper. "Leave me alone too. Your slithering ways are detestable, you are incapable of loving, nurturing, or providing any true sustenance. You speak of my greed and believe your love is loyal and will never betray me. Ha! The love I have with Miss Tolemy is unlike the treacherous love that breeds inside you. Leave this place. Leave me alone. Leave us alone!"

"Louis? I asked you a question." Miss Tolemy spoke with a note of impatience. "Do I need to make myself clearer? Louis what is it? What is it you see when you stare at me? Do you even see me? Louis!"

"Yes Miss Tolemy. I can see you. But the paper? What about the paper?" "

I have said all I need to say about the paper, which brings me to my other point."

"Other point?" I reflected. Suddenly feeling that I could not be certain of anything. "I have considered organizing a tutor to work with you. This, I believe, will improve your grades considerably. Now would this be something you would be interested in?"

"Yes, Miss Tolemy. Why would I not do anything you suggest on my behalf?"

"Good," she paused, looking somewhat confused by my selected vocabulary. "But now we are out of time. Could you come back after school so we can finish this conversation?"

"Yes Miss Tolemy. I will be here just like before."

"Before?" she asked looking even more confused. "In any case, I will see you after school."

"I knew she would come to me again," I said under my breath as I quietly left the classroom. I was thrilled that she had invited me back after school as she had done before. Still, I pondered over the possible discourse that was to come. I feared the return of the Snake. Moloch! Would it interfere again and talk of a past that I could not understand? If that happened, I would be prepared. I would turn away from its crawling belly and deceptive forked tongue which continuously tries to destroy my love for Miss Tolemy. I would not let it remove my flesh from her nurturing bosom. I would squash its will to undermine our love. Our chosen love for one another. I will not let you. I will fight you! I will erase all thoughts of you! Yes, this is what I will do!

"Truly, Louis, this is your utterly exhaustive plan to remove me from you? You should know better. By now you should be fully in tune with the fallacy of your own words which denote your own meaningless rants. But you are not in tune. You understand nothing. Nothing Louis, that is without me!"

"Then we shall see!" I responded before dismissing the thought.

I counted down the seconds until the bell marked the end of another school day. When finally, I met with my beloved teacher.

"Thank you for staying back after school. Louis." She spoke from across her desk.

"Now as per my earlier suggestion on tutoring I have a former advanced student who is willing to work with you twice a week after school. Now is this something you are willing to do?"

While registering her words, my eyes were distracted by the formation of her tender lips as she spoke. I wanted to stretch across her desk and place my own lips on hers.

"Louis, stop staring at me and just answer the question!"

"Yes Miss Tolemy, of course. I am willing to do whatever you want. Anything!"

"Alright then, I am glad you are receptive to this idea."

"Of course, I would do whatever you thought best for us. Only, could this tutoring be held at another place? Perhaps you could tutor on my behalf?"

"Another place?" she flatly interjected. "It will take place here at school and I cannot tutor you. I have already been given the heads up from my former student who is willing to work with you. Is that clear enough?"

"Here at school? But I need you to tutor me and from another place. A place not far from here."

"Excuse me Louis. The answer is no. You will meet your tutor here in this classroom and not at some other place." As she shot me a strange look I could not decipher.

"No teacher, this is all wrong!"

Only now her expression was now laced with a harder edge as I felt the distance growing rapidly between us. I could only watch disbelief as she alienated herself from me. Any earlier settings that we were previously aligned to were now thwarted with new conditions. Unlike any prior surroundings.

But I wasn't going to give up so easily.

"Miss Tolemy, perhaps you have forgotten this place that is not far from here?" However, when she didn't respond, anxiety began to set in as I now desperately wanted her to remember the address that had brought us so much happiness. Surely the mention of the address alone would bring back her lost and treasured memories. "1010 Lotus Way!"

"Lotus Way? I do not know such an address Louis and have forgotten nothing. However now I believe we are done here. We will discuss your tutoring schedule when the time is more appropriate for you. Now good day," she said before getting up to leave.

Good day? She spoke where now I could feel the flesh of her soul instantly departing from me. Before my very eyes. An anguish beginning to penetrate itself throughout me. A suffering I had never known.

"No," I began to plead "Do not do that. Do not hide from me and take away what you have given. A love only we served. How could you forsake me and the existence only we inhabited? This world can go on without me. As now I'm torn and reduced to mere atoms that will exist without needs, thoughts, desires. Please do not go! Cease to be seen and to touch your flesh no more. Smell your skin's dew when morning rises. Taste your lips when night falls. Please... Please do not go!"

"Who Stands Close By"

Only her love did slip away from me, and as the weeks drifted slowly by I longed for her return. One day she'll come back, I tried to reassure myself. Come back to 1010 Lotus Way where our love once dwelt. Where her flowing white gown first summoned me to her balcony. Only now where are those late sunny afternoons from where now only disharmony strikes? What has happened to my lover whose strong blue eyes conveyed meaning and passion? What happened to my lover? What happened to us?

"Yes, Louis, what has become of us? Befallen while I have always stood alongside you. Giving you counsel. What happened to Louis? Where only Miss Tolemy's guidance you suddenly sought. While now you are without remembrance. You have forgotten me. You have forgotten us."

"You are a crafty one aren't you? Have I called upon you? No! Yet your betrayal always lingers. I have never sought your counsel. The Voice is my lone instructor. Not you! Never Snake whose knowledge only divides and tears away. For you are a servant of disorder and discord along a continued destruction."

"Dummy! I am the Voice. The Voice you summon and seek as your provider and protector. My generosity was unconditionally when I gave you the teacher, but now you have denied me but not her. No, teacher this and teacher that and only more teacher. Yes, she I have given, though now will I take from you!"

"No Moloch! You are mistaken in your judgment. You didn't give the teacher to me. She gave herself willingly, I walked to 1010 Lotus Way where she welcomed me. Her love and devotion were real. Every week her crystal blue eyes would touch my soul. Our lips would taste one another's. Our union came to fruition because Miss Tolemy and I allowed it to. Not you who bleeds from disfigurement and disillusionment."

"My dear Louis, how is it you persist in your own error? Perhaps you are misinformed by some other unsound source. However, now I speak to you with only good intentions. From a just cause. For now there is one who stands near you. Close by. Your betrayer. A lone antagonist. A foe you must learn and stand before."

"Only now spare me your psychobabble. An adversary other than yourself near me? What a joke! A breeder of lies is what you are."

"Defiance might make you feel satisfied with yourself, but the charges you bring against me are unfair. For I do not lie to you out of mere jest. Nor do I deceive you unless it is best for you. You see, I protect you from any ill-fated truths that could bring you harm. However, what I tell you next is no lie. It will open your eyes to see my goodwill and you will call upon me once more. If it is her you want, then she will I give back."

"Give her back? Only what trickery is this you now carry out on my behalf?"

"Your lover Louis. Your Miss Tolemy. She has found another to replace you."

"Replace me? Look, just go away. Get away from me!"

"I cannot do that. This you already know. However, the truth remains your lover is with someone else. Who seeks out the same address as you once did yourself. 1010 Lotus Way is where your enemy lays his head."

"Truth? Whose truth? Yours? For only does she love me but if it ever be so I shall find her again. One like her. Someone untainted, who doesn't try to coerce me like you do. Now leave. Leave me at once!"

"Find another? Really Louis. Now who is delusional? Only that pale feeble creature you walk along the corridors with will ever yield to your unusual needs."

"Then she will remain as you say? Miss Tolemy will come back to me."

"She will if I allow it. It will happen if you stand your ground with this one adversary, this enemy who is stealing your lover away from you."

"Then who? Who am I to pursue as my adversary?"

"He is closer than you think. However first you need to observe and learn his ways. The high school is where you will find him, but the school's parking lot is where you will witness his wrongdoings. His transgressional misdeeds sworn against you. Against us. It is also where you will find Miss Tolemy."

I carefully mused over the origin from where this advice came. Knowing Moloch's cunning habits I wasn't convinced that I had been given wise advice. The Snake was insincere and it wasn't unusual for him to Use Compassionate counsel to disguise his impure stratagems.

Two can play at that game, I thought.

"Maybe I don't care anymore. I said, testing the waters. I'd much rather forget your existence that entraps me continually. 'Let this 'other' have her. I don't need to endure any further devastating repercussions from what you have already laid out for me. I don't need your misguided sympathies. I don't trust you. Just leave me."

"Again Louis, I cannot do that. I cannot leave - from a birth that formed our eternal union. Now your adversary is near."

How I knew those words to be true. An eternal unification though one to which I never endeavored upon. While accepting any anguish from whose authority disables me. Ignoring my own pleas to forget while somehow continuing forward through its rant on my behalf.

"Does not pride call out to you Louis? Does shame and a trembling heart now shroud your judgment? I'm speaking to you. Do you hide behind the coward's maternal bosom when you should face your foes with an unshrinking fearlessness? Napoleon-Caesar's undaunting valor endures within you. You must honor this. Victory awaits but dishonor infects you. Maybe your loss of Miss Tolemy is worth the discomfort of an ignoble existence which will soon inhabit you?"

"Only what then? What can I do?" I found myself desperately pleading with my perpetual enemy. From where now her repeated invitations lie lost. Where the past only layers itself against me.

"I will give you the name Louis. I will offer it to you. You will then seek him out and upon finding him inflict a lawful revenge."

"The name?" I uttered aloud.

"Yes, the name."

"To avenge my honor and pride." I now counseled myself into believing. "Yes, give me the name of this unworthy foe. The name, Snake!!" *"Winston. This is your betrayer's name. Winston Rumstitch. That two-bit, nothing wood shop teacher who cannot even deliver proper foreplay to a lover who consumes you day and night. An unpleasant accident in the woodshop however could be his undoing."*

"Winston Rumstitch?" I said in disbelief.

"Yes Louis. The man who is fucking your lover right now."

"That gauntly, owl-eyed, wiry wood shop teacher? I asked, puzzled by the thought. "This can't be! You are lying and trying to trick me. The Voice will speak the truth. For her ways remain benevolent. She would never harm me. This time I shall Leave and quickly depart from you!"

"The Voice! You fool! I am its Voice. No distinction lies between us for we are the same. I will however grant you this wish. I will meander away but I will still dwell close by. You will call upon me again when you call upon the Voice. Your benevolent Voice!"

Hence I quickly summoned the Voice. "It is Louis. Your friend who now seeks proper counsel. Where are you? Can you not hear me?" I asked again, wondering if the Snake had reared its ugly head and taken her away from me. As Cain had taken from his own flesh, lying patiently only to slay his own brother's blood. "Where is your prudence I desire? Where virtue does not conceal itself as it hides deep inside the Snake."

"Here I am. Beside you always. My brother did not silently wait to place his sword against me. I should think not!" He and I are one. We are

one Louis. Conceived from the same womb. Brother killing brother? What sort of delusionary mind is this you speak from?"

"Have you never heard of this ancient old crime? Cain Killing Abel? Brother against brother?!"

"Perhaps this narrative has crossed my path. While now I should remember this mortal act from a time long ago. From the creation of time." "Yes, that's right, it's biblical. From its first book, Genesis. This cruel madness from a brother whose hands were stained with his brother's own blood."

"Yes, now I remember. Though I should think his madness comes from a greater sin. A jealousy that ruled Cain's misguided Conduct. A sin as old as mankind itself."

"Envy was ultimately Cain's ruin when he killed his own brother. A deplorable act yet this sin of envy can fester inside the very bowels of men and women alike. Until at last it erupts and madness takes hold. But first the seed of envy must plant itself: planning, deceiving, Coveting brother and sister and neighbor alike. This is the origin from where Cain's madness began and from there the unspeakable act he committed."

"You speak with truth and seem to have an intimate understanding of jealousy's affliction. But am I to believe that anyone could be struck with this single state of mind?"

"Truly, you ask important questions. Yes, anyone could easily be stricken with this malady. You see, the teacher was my gift to you. Only now that she has been taken from you I will carefully plant my jealous seed inside you."

"Inside my own flesh where envy will overpower any reason? Only I am not Cain who holds such peculiar distinctions as I could never slay my own brother, my flesh, another, human being. There must be another way to rid my enemy." I tried to make sense of the situation.

Something simple yet as effective as spilling the blood of another being. I continued to muse over. Perhaps I could spread lies? Accusations of shame that would take over the intruder. Hence, offering a now sworn enemy no other choice but to resign and leave Miss Tolemy. Although a bribe may be more effective in encouraging his ultimate departure. A bribe of some substantial worth. Only possessing such wealth would prove more than outside my means. What if something better than gold could be offered? A bribe of another source? Another woman perhaps. A night lady and then he could lose his body, mind and soul to another woman and leave my lover altogether. Only where would I find a woman like this? A lady of the night.

"Idle rumors... Bribes... Ladies of the night... You fool! The idiocies that spill from your mouth are absurd. Who do you think Winston Rumstitch slept with before enjoying the company of your beloved Miss Tolemy? *"Ladies of the night" you idiot. Regardless, the options you present are only temporal Solutions that won't help you in the long run. Pathetic is what you are. This is why I must talk to you so vehemently to get through your imbecile nature. Only you continue to refuse my good counsel as your ears do not hear. Why did Cain Kill his brother? JEALOUSY. And from the bowels of his jealous wrath did Abel perish and from the same fate that now awaits Winston."*

"Cain's jealous madness is to be your madness, Louis, You must rid us of this problem. Permanently. Give no quarter. No return is possible."

"No return?" I asked as a sudden chill shot up my spine. "Where life can no longer sustain itself? Where love and hate perish simultaneously? What then? I become a ruthless murderer. You are mistaken to believe I am so callous; I will not kill him. Now leave me Snake and offer this madness to someone else!"

"Someone else? Only you exist alongside me. You are not thinking rationally. I assure you that I am not implying that you carry out some senseless act. No Louis, Napoleon-Caesar fought and killed under the requirements of the laws. In the name of liberation, both men used rule and order to defend just causes. Unlike the lawless disorder and anarchy which is demonstrated inside unruly ghettos or the minds of paranoid schizophrenic megalomaniacs."

"But you are asking me to end one's life. I will not extinguish a life from its natural course. Hence, I will choose. Choose not to accompany your unnatural and demented ideas on the destruction of others. I have no Use for you. Now go away!"

"Dummy! Why is it you insist upon frustrating your lone companion and sole instrument of enlightenment? You have already been chosen. Louis. Selected as Napoleon and Caesar had been by an intelligent body who wanted its people to be empowered and unified. It was an acceptable system that eradicated riffraff and anarchistic vermin." "And if I suppose this to be true and Napoleon-Caesar did not uproot cities and states in the name of anarchy?" I now closely examined from the Snake's own tongue. "Instead a functional system of structural efficiency. A well-defined methodical autocracy void of any piracy subduing all barbarism, harmful revolutionists, undesirables, and alliances who threatened the empire itself."

"Yes Louis. Now you are beginning to clearly see!"

Moloch spoke with more approval as I continued. "People like Winston Rumstitch cannot satisfy the needs of the Napoleonic-Caesarism order because they are unfit and unworthy. The empire must come first. Winston unlawfully stole Miss Tolemy and from the empire. He stole from me!"

"Yes Louis, the empire's needs must come first unlike Winston's whose condition proves disruptive and agitating to the people. You must strike Louis! For truly does your lover and he always enter and leave the school together."

I considered the accusation. "Did it ever occur to you that they may just be traveling together to and from school to save money? A practical means of transportation?"

"You really are clueless and in denial. Go on. Keep telling yourself what you want to hear but it will get you nowhere. Do not wait until it's too late. You must strike. Strike and bring peace back to the empire once more."

Its words struck a chord in me. I didn't want to lose my beloved. My beloved who belonged to the empire. "Okay, then I must. I will lay low and follow his every step, every movement, and every breath until it is his last!"

"Mr. Rumstitch"

"Good afternoon class. Welcome to second semester woodshop where home economics is outlawed, and proper grammar does not apply." He smiled through the thicket of his mustache. "I see most of you have come back from last semester but you in the back corner? Have you attended my class before? You look familiar but I seem to have misplaced your name."

Of course I look familiar, I wanted to say aloud but thought better of it and clenched my lips instead. Patience was paramount. And why should you have misplaced my name? You imbecile. What a fool you are to take Miss Tolemy from me and the empire! When you lie next to her and close your eyes, remember that the eyes of the empire never close and never sleep!

"It was the ninth, maybe the tenth grade when you last attended my class. Leopold?"

"My name is Louis." I answered, taking in my rival's oversized eyes which sank into his skull. On the contrary, his ears stuck out like mug handles. His mustache was unkempt like his dark hair.

"And you are Winston who taught me in the ninth grade."

"Forgive me, Louis, now I remember," he said as his eyes curiously scanned over me. "Anyway, it's good to have you back in my class again."

"Now as most of you should already know my name is Mr. Rumstitch, and I will be your woodshop teacher for this new semester. Well then…" he said rubbing his hands together, "if there is nothing else, let's get started. Now, to maintain a safe environment: the rules are of utmost importance. Who can tell me the very first rule we all must follow?" His deep-set eyes swept the room as he waited for a response.

"I see the same show of hands from last semester, but what about you Louis? Can you remember our number one woodshop rule?"

Keep your filthy hands off my Miss Tolemy, I thought glaring at his bony, calloused hands. Your days of finger fucking my Miss Tolemy are going to abruptly end. I may be generous and leave you with eight fingers. But I will be taking your two finger-fucking fingers away from you and I'll watch as the blood drips from your own blade. Or maybe I'll leave you with none. A fingerless man with only palms. My rightful lover will surely reject you then. You will sit with old men in the park who are too feeble to fight alongside their devoted country men. Moreover, you will spend your anguished hours with those who cannot walk anymore or feed themselves. Your mind will be rendered useless and ineffectual.

I savored the image and felt power surging through me. My fingers would remain intact and my strength would prevail. I had made a pledge to my alliance and there was no turning back. I would make my mark and I would make it soon.

"Louis? Are you still with us back there?" Mr. Rumstitch asked, clicking his despicable fingers together to get my attention.

"The first rule of safety is..."

"To keep your fingers away from the blade," I said, snapping out of my daze.

"That is sound advice, Louis. Always, Safety first. His speech faded strangely from me. However, that's not the answer I am looking for here. Can anyone else tell me this first rule that everyone needs to obey?"

"Mr. Rumstitch!" I cried out from the corner, knowing this show was only between the two of us and I'd soon be wearing his blood.

"Safety glasses. Every student must wear safety glasses before operating machinery in your woodshop!"

"Good Louis Very good! You remember!"

"Yes, I do. I certainly remember Mr. Rumstitch."

"The Parking Lot"

At last the school's final bell rang and I immediately set out to the parking lot. I bided my time thinking about Mr. Rumstitch's burning lust for my woman which only enraged me more. My enthusiasm escalated to new heights as I silently waited at a distance, just far enough to observe my enemy. I knew Miss Tolemy would emerge by his side but I didn't blame her. I had examined this strange, fruitless union and knew she had been coerced. A reckless love grown rooted from every deceptive practice. A bad seed he had planted in her heart. Winston and him alone was to blame. I was sure of that. He was accountable and he would pay.

Thus, I waited! Though supposing my only plan was to wait as I was not entirely clear how he would pay. However, I was confident that it would unfold as it should. When my unworthy opponent made himself visible any instinctive actions would quickly become realized. Hence, I followed the stream of students from the school's rear exit until a mere trickle remained. Finally, each teacher stepped out. Soon, I told myself, from the laden breaths I drew in and from the equally heavy breaths I released.

My eyes continued to stay vigilant from afar when suddenly his undeniable presence was in view. Walking alongside Miss Tolemy, his gauntly frame struggled to carry the protruding bump on his weary back, I cringed to see them together in the afternoon sun which rightfully belonged to me and Miss Tolemy. Although I had seen them walking together on other occasions, I had not known his true means until now. While now how much more closer he walks beside her. How much more fearlessly he casts away the school's watchful eye.

Without another thought I began to march, then stepped boldly inside a passage to anticipate my next move. Euphoria tried to course through me but the feeling was weighed down by uncertainty. For I didn't know what would prevail and feared that my fighting skills would prove less than adequate. As an afterthought, I decided it would be best to search the parking lot for a formidable makeshift weapon. Though soon to quickly realize my now narrowed vision was targeting him and only him.

"Think," I began to command myself, aloud as I drew near my adversary. "Think," I repeatedly told myself.

"My hands!" I at last, envisioned, "I will show him what my bare hands are capable of and I will plunge my fingers into his throat with precision and unrelenting pressure. I will close his airway from where he breathes life into him. Yes, that is what I will do."

"Dummy! That is not what you will do!" Its voice resurfaced once again as my unbroken steps grew closer to Winston. "Behave like some lunatic maniac. You will stop now."

"Why should I stop?" I asked inwardly. "Because of your authority? Your misguided ways? I will not stop! Besides, didn't you already put me in charge of disposing this refuse? My adversary? Now you want to refute your own instructions. This is ludicrous! You are the madman lunatic."

"Am I, or is it you whose understanding escapes you? Certainly, we must remove this refuse from us, but not with the method you have in mind. You do not yet possess the strength nor mindset to pull this off. You will not proceed with this mindless plan. You will stop now!"

And somehow through this unexpected submission I stopped. Ceasing my own objective. I never really wanted to carry out this order of elimination in the first place. Perhaps the memories of my lover would quickly fade or maybe the Snake had a better plan. It always had one more. More deceptive and cruel from all previous proposals,

Nevertheless, I discarded my course of action and began to listen to the Snake, Moloch. It's malign words now echoing through me.

"Hear my instruction Louis. Haste has no advantage here. While we must rid ourselves from this man of wood, your misguided plot of strangulation will not do. You have never taken another life. Whereas I have. I have destroyed many men great and small. Women and children too, as well as their hopes and dreams. There was no hesitation in destroying what posterity had already decided for them."

"But I am willing to prove you wrong, Snake. This man is not of my caliber. His bones are blanketed by flesh like an old cadaver."

"You will not pursue this. His so-called cadaverous flesh and determined mind will eventually overpower you. Even if you have the upper hand it will require sustainable strength to achieve an ultimate outcome. While your hands and fingers crush his throat, you will not squeeze out his last breath. He will refuse to be the victim and will fight incessantly to defend his life. He will fight for survival, whether you think he is worthy or not. In the end, you will fall short Louis. You need to strike with an approach that has been effective for even the weakest of men."

"So, now you insult me, even though you abide right alongside me. Tell me Snake.... reveal to me this grandiose undertaking. This plan where I will seize power through vengeance."

"This is not as difficult as you believe. You think too much yet overlook everything. Fast and swift is how you must strike. An immediate confrontation with blitzkrieg, lightning speed. This is how Napoleon-Caesar executed battle: the opposition is oblivious to attack until it is too late. Only then will your foe and loyal enemy become aware of his surroundings, his mortal fate."

"What then? What instrument will bring the kind of death you seek? A gun? Certainly a gun would bring a quick ending. A death of "lightning speed" as you put it."

"A gun will not do, nor will another weapon that is used at any given distance. The instrument must be more personal. An implement which will be felt by both you and your adversary. Something that will yoke you together. The suffering will begin on your first strike. When you pierce

his skin you will feel your own flesh clasping against the cold instrument. And as the cold steel penetrates deeper inside him you will draw power from his last breath."

"Only why?" I asked the devious one. "Why should I deliver this kind of pain? This misery? Then take his last remaining breath on Earth? Why Snake? Is it not enough that his body will lie still forever? Or perhaps it's your own pleasure you seek. The greater the performance the more satiable you become."

"Why are you always overthinking on my behalf? Take heed of what I am telling you. This man of wood took your thoughts and desires from you and callously destroyed them. His heartless behavior deserves your utmost retaliation. An eye for an eye. His suffering in exchange of your own. Complete revenge requires you to feel his pain. This is how you will garner strength. An absolute, unbridled retribution whereupon the state becomes whole once again."

"Then I shall!" I began to carefully reflect. I shall seek his pain. A pain he so recklessly inflicted upon me. His very suffering will replace the pain I have endured.

"But where would I find such an instrument that is capable of satisfying these mortally lethal requirements?" I asked, standing in the midst of a now empty parking lot. I wondered what type of weapon I would use that was both versatile and lethal. I imagined wielding a polished sword in all its chivalry. My faithful determination against my foe would be deemed worthy by the state and I would be accepted for my loyal courage.

"Tell me Snake, the name of this worthy implement that I will use under your command?"

"With a knife and sword, pike and dagger you will choose from this arsenal I give you. These weapons will vanquish the false strength that your enemy boasts. He will be hopeless as there will be no chance of him having any advantage over you. You will remove all fortitude and resistance. He will be without."

"Yes, an enemy without. Only what weapon should I displace my enemy with? For now you speak in various tongues. A pointed edged dagger, or a sword would suffice. Then again, I could use a medieval pike to strike my enemy down. I would skillfully manipulate the whole of the linear shaft to crush all existing life from him. What Snake? What weapon should I use?"

"Patience Louis. You must diligently wait for the knowledge you seek. An awakening will occur. From your own darkness you will soar high into the sunlit skies where the ruling scepter of Napoleon-Caesar will touch you. It will embrace you! Then, and only then will you see everything around you. Carefully biding your time while obediently pursuing your purpose. Our purpose, Louis, and under my instruction then the executioner will come to lay his heavy hand against his foe, Rumstitch. The man of wood and anyone else who gets in its way."

"A Flawless Machine"

So I obeyed. Surrendering to the Snake's tongue through hours of endless waiting. Anxiously standing by until its appearance, Moloch, would welcome me once more. Although hatred for the calculating creature remained I could not break my alliance with it. For now I knew its ways and its direct path to Miss Tolemy. Without Moloch I would be without her forever. Even though the Snake was more vile, more cunning, more insincere, it was from these deficient qualities I now sought corrupt standards to which could bring down my rival. Never would Winston stand between us again and I would take back what already belonged to me. My lover, Miss Tolemy. Realizing at the same time the Voice could not lead me through this battle of reprisal. Unlike the Snake, the Voice remained a limited creature: without hate, without violence to instruct my path against him, Winston. Holding mere pacifying habits countering those of the Snake.

Thus, from these truths I would turn to the allegiance of the Snake whose commanding tongue I could no longer ignore. Its friendship, however, I would continue to stay far away.

Soon I would find myself behind the school's parking lot again. It had become common practice for me to observe my enamored enemy who continuously coerced my lover into his vehicle each and every day after school. Hence, would I call upon its emergence daily to seek out instruction. But it would only offer silence as I watched in constant my woman entering the woodman's driving machine. Unlike the pathetic qualities which imbued Winston, my wretched enemy, his car was exceptional, giving him a false sense of identity. I detested his smug face as he drove away with my girl in his brilliant black Lincoln Mark V. A flawless machine properly chromed from front to back and side to side. A time machine standing still through its formidable cold steel and romantic appeal.

"Who does Winston think he is?" I asked myself, hoping the Snake would respond. "Some childish fictitious superhero driving his super mobile?"

Yet there she was. My lover alongside him. The only solace I could find were thoughts of my enemy's impending doom. I imagined the fatality taking place right here in the parking lot, where I found myself each and every day waiting for the Snake's next command.

"Only why? Why now?" I asked myself. "Why does its tongue lie dormant? Slithering back into its dark hole. Silently abiding inside its selfish cause."

I wondered if the Snake was perhaps commanding me through its soundless abyss. Subconsciously its silent tongue may be giving me order and direction. Instruction on my behalf.

Perhaps I should observe more diligently and take notice of all elements around me. I realized that I needed to map out my own battlefield. To do this, I needed to interpret the Snake's mute tongue.

Only now, as I continued to look on, I still could not identify the direct means of action to take on this vehicular battlefield of asphalt. Without the Snake's direct guidance, the task of planning any comprehensive action proved difficult, so I considered the arena I'd been given. Thoughtfully surveying the grounds as Napoleon-Caesar would have done, I realized that the call for action would present itself in time. The most destructive design would arrive through reconnaissance and patience.

The tolling bell marked another day's end and I once again marched out to my usual spot in the parking lot, waiting for it to speak. Hoping its tongue, Moloch, would relish an opportunity once more as now days turned into weeks. However, I knew my day would come. It would differ from all other days where now I only kept watch on students and teachers as they exited the building of indoctrination.

Yes, soon that day would come and present another stage, another purpose. The arena would be set and a new momentum of force and provocation would guide me. I would submit to this internal power without any means of reason or thought.

In my hopeful search for answers, I had mindlessly walked over to the school's Football field. Piece by piece I began to watch the field's surrounding battered old chain link fence come down. Each fencing, with each rusted post extracted from its hole. Uncertain of it all. Wondering if this location fitted into the greater scheme of things. Although Moloch had not spoken for some time, I instinctively sensed that its instruction was near.

Hence, I obediently watched the pile of fencing grow higher alongside the increasing heap of elongated steel posts uprooted from the ground. I watched and then I went home.

"Pike and Dagger"

Having fed my tired body, I immediately retired to my bedroom. I tried to sleep but my thoughts would only continue to revisit the dismantling of the chain link fence. Gradually however, my thoughts wandered elsewhere, into a labyrinth of dark commands. Where its tongue held sovereignty over me, luring me deeper into its realm. Exhausting me where at last sleep took hold of me.

Sleep, from through a dream it's apparition would speak to me. Its rant cutting through my restless thoughts until I awoke in darkness repeating its words.

"Knife and sword, Pike and dagger." I repeated the Snake's words until a clear vision presented itself to me: The chain link fence and its purpose.

While neither a sharpened blade nor a polished sword could be fashioned from that cold fence, the metal posts however...

Yes, the extended shaft of the posts, I concluded.

The elongated pike will become my chosen weapon.

Now I understood that a metal post had been handpicked for me. Even though it didn't have a sharpened point, its spear-like velocity would be a capable implement to crush any life it touched.

I will hold the shaft perpendicular, I continued my reflection through the darkness. Neatly cupped inside the pit of my arm until I'm ready to strike.

I imagined myself standing like a soldier inside a phalanx of Alexander's great armies. My breath heavy as my disruptor emerges in his black machine. Rapidly accelerating, its momentum now my ally as I begin to run toward him. Pike extended and from one exact measured moment I lunge upwards. The pike's strength carrying me forward and through the shattering windshield of my victim's black target. Collapsing all life inside to which my enemy once knew.

Yes, I thought with assurance. I will now wait for your command, Snake. Your command to pick up pike and dagger!

However as the days grew longer, the Snake's silence grew louder. It would not even speak to me through my dreams. Its peculiar game was more maddening than ever before. While its incessant clamor was not missed, I longed for our dubious companionship.

How cunningly evil can Moloch the Snake be? I wondered. I thought we had a pact.

While I mused over possible reasons for its absence, I was sure of one thing: the Snake knew how to recognize an opportune moment and select the right time and place for action. I thought about the one command it had given me, "Pick up the pike!" But what next?

"What then?" I asked with weary patience. "What command am I truly waiting for? Why do you lie dormant inside me now? Why should I even count on you? You don't rule the state and certainly not the whole of the empire."

It seemed to me that the Snake had laid out for itself an undeserving autocracy. Lining itself, alongside Napoleon-Caesar. Believing that one day it would overthrow the Napoleonic-Caesarism reign. But I knew deep down that Moloch's sovereignty held itself over me and me alone. But it had always been an unwanted yoke and I needed to cast it from off me.

I decided that I would not wait for Moloch's reply. I would move forward toward my objective independently. Satisfying my own commands that the crown would deem worthy. I would remove from its realm any flawed populace. Where by proficiently eliminating those who impede upon its hegemony and only cripple its impetus prowess.

Yes, I will banish all the blemished people who have no right. People whose image approximates Winston's.

From this revelation I now had understanding. My instruction would arise directly from the empire and its Napoleonic-Caesarism reign. Not from one who crawls on its stomach and who believes in its superiority from those above. Recklessly including itself inside the celestial bodies where the heavens command. Where the infinite dominion of Napoleon-Caesar looks down. When soon, I thought, they will look down upon me and not the Snake.

Thus, I made my decision to serve the authority which reigns from above. Then I waited for that auspicious day to arrive. Only this would be no ordinary day but one which would deliver a final outcome for both Winston and I.

Only now I needed to train myself to use this weapon that had been chosen from the realm above!

The following day after school I found myself staring down at the pile of metal posts. My eyes swept over the entangled heap as I quickly discovered that most of the old metal was corroded. But I was not going to be deterred by the exterior of this seemingly useless mass, I began to probe inside the top layers, deconstructing the pyramid of metal posts one by one. When finally my perseverance was rewarded as it had taken all of one hour to uncover that one invincible instrument. Seemingly unscathed from the other, eroded metal posts surrounding it. For its end was surprisingly untouched as my preying hands now found just enough shaft to clench onto.

Pulling with all the inner strength I could muster, the chosen one slowly began to free itself.

"Pull," I charged myself. "Pull!"

Suddenly I was stumbling backwards though at the same time realizing the would be weapon was still securely in my hands. As I regained my footing I immediately began to examine its long and heavy tubular structure which at first felt clumsy inside my redeeming hands. Though unlike the other eroded posts, this one was well preserved. I marveled over how it had not deteriorated. As if polished silver and not zinc bonded its tubular body. While protecting it from every unkind element that nature could afflict. It was as if the post had been shielded all those years, waiting for me alone to seize it.

Thus, I would train myself to use this six-foot instrument of death. An impromptu vision I set out to manifest as I held onto its crude, cold feel. While it owned no speared head, its long formidable shaft and powerful weight proved more than satisfying. It was the medieval pike I would now align myself with. Creating an anatomy that extended from my own, the pike would coexist as one with me. The posterior of this deadly shaft would be hidden under my jacket while I kept my distance from any potential admirers. Then I would expose my fearless weapon to Winston.

I believed that my paradoxical actions would prove their worth without raising suspicion. While in full view I would wait for those to pass me by before fulfilling my intentions. Only then would any interference be too late.

Only now I had to map out a strategic plan and selectively choose the battlefield that would await both Winston and I. Though uncertain at first, I suddenly realized what was before me. On the other side of the parking lot a short bend before a long stretch of road, leading to the town's main street.

"A clear, straight and narrow path," I now carefully thought aloud. "This stretch will give me the distance I need to increase both Winston's speed and that from my own two legs."

Only today would not be that day where any plan of execution was hastened. As I found myself staring at the pike, then I looked up.

It was him. The man of wood and my lover were leaving the school building. They were walking toward his black Lincoln Mark V. It was his only prized possession as Miss Tolemy did not belong to him. She was mine, and mine alone. But today would not be one of reckoning. Tomorrow, I told myself, as I quickly noted the time. 4:15 p.m.

It was a cloudless Monday afternoon and when everyone left the school grounds I practiced moves with my pike. It was almost dark when I left the metal pile to go home.

"Stop!"

Today, I told myself, imagining Mr. Rumstitch when he would collide with my pike. This was my last class for the day and I counted down the minutes. I hoped this would be the very last time I laid my eyes on him.

"Louis. Stop staring at me and get those safety glasses on." Suddenly he was near.

"Louis!"

"Yes Mr. Rumstitch. Today!"

"No, not today. Now! Put those glasses on immediately Louis," he bellowed, rolling his owlish eyes.

As he turned from me to tend to another student, my thoughts turned from him. I imagined a scene I would rejoice, over and over again. My Miss Tolemy, my lover. Today I would rescue her from an unwanted love. One she never longed for.

Today she will lay my naked body down and command her will over me as before. Today everything will change, but nothing will change at all. For this love has always belonged to me. To us.

When at last the slow moving minutes of another day concluded as I found myself once again mingled with students quickly leaving the school's building. My mind was numb as I broke free from the crowd, and made my way to the pyramid of eroded metal posts.

My sole attention was on searching behind the mangled heap where my pike was hidden. Once it was back in my hands, I felt its redeeming strength as I had the previous day.

I quickly took note of the time 3:11 p.m. Again, it was sunny without a cloud in the sky.

I refocused my attention on the pike and visualized how it could seal my fate along with my enemy's. Then I hastily set out toward my last stand. Walking through the parking lot with weapon on shoulder, I passed cars and students who paid no attention as they made their way out of the school boundaries. At last, I passed the short bend where the straight stretch began.

While continuing my redeeming march I stopped at midpoint.

A distance I assessed that was still in proximity to the lingering students and teachers. I continued until I reached the town's main street. It seemed far enough away from any curious eyes, but it was too far from the parking lot. I reconsidered my position.

I needed to be less detectable, but I also needed to keep my target in sight. I headed back, near midpoint, then carefully surveyed the area. The shorter distance would thwart my reaction time, yet I was confident that I could rely on my battlefield instincts and use this distance to my advantage.

Without another thought my watchful eyes withdrew from the parking lot to observe cars slowing down as they proceeded to the bend. One by one, each car slowly made its way around this impediment before accelerating onto the straight where I now stood. Soon Winston's black driving machine would come through...

I stood like a soldier by the narrow straight, clenching onto the pike's cold exterior. Eagerly waiting for its command to draw arms and strike, but ignorant taunts began to recklessly disrupt me at the same time.

"Look y'all," one said, turning to his passengers. "Louis thinks he's in the king's army!"

"The track and Field team needs a good javelin thrower Louis!" said another heckler.

"Is that your make-believe gun? Stand to attention sergeant." A giggling cheerleader said, saluting from a back seat.

I let their taunts slide as I knew that one day their scorn would be replaced with praise and servitude. Like Winston, they did not fear their own erroneous ways. Positioning themselves inside subdivisions while demonstrating their disloyalties to one another.

Though from each growing taunt would I continue my fervent watch of the road's bend even more so. Each driving machine clearly inside my vision. Their faces, however uncertain until each driver drew near. But I was sure I would register the treacherous face of my enemy, even from afar. And unlike each tiresome vehicle that drove through this convenient impediment, Winston's own machine was anything but mundane, with its sleek, black, distinguishable finish that boasted a brilliant hemmed chrome from front to back. For although he now parades himself inside this masquerade of pretentious lies his pompous edge would not last for long. Soon his own lies would unleash his own destruction from a strike uncoiling itself inside lightning like speed and from my own blitzkrieg. Miss Tolemy would bear witness to this punitive action, but she would turn to me once more. Whereupon realizing her own infidelities against state and empire. Against me!

But I would forgive Cleo Tolemy for her misgivings.

I will hold her without blame because my love is true.

In contrast, Winston's romantic intentions were meticulously deceitful. From a trickery forged by his own actions. While now my zealous heart only craved retribution.

As I looked to the sky, I savored the thought of reuniting with my lover. The sun now hid behind the clouds and an eerie backdrop surrounded me. I checked the time and realized there was little point in doing so. My moment had finally arrived.

Traveling through a space towards the path's bend, I captured the elegant Lincoln Mark V, its unmistakable outline slowly inching closer. My heart began to race, and my limbs trembled as I beseeched my arms and legs to remain steady. Adrenaline pumping fast throughout me with a level of intensity and anticipation I had previously failed to imagine! Next, I heard its silent command to draw arms. I obeyed. Aiming the pike at my sworn enemy just as I had envisioned. Producing the deadly shaft, some five feet from my body, I embedded both feet onto the battleground. My own phantom phalanx.

The black machine slowly exited the bend to where I stood. Where turning back had become an impossibility for both my enemy and I. Not now, not ever. As the thought gave me the strength to steady my mind and body. However, something wasn't right. This scene wasn't the one I had imagined. As I looked through Winston's windshield, the unbending script which had formed in my mind now suddenly gave way to confusion.

Where is she? I asked myself gaping at the only shadowy figure sitting in the driver's seat. He's alone? Isn't she always by his side?

This was unexpected to say the least. Every day I watch them both leave the school together. Why was this day any different?

A distant feeling began to suddenly take over. A restless uneasiness telling me all was not as it should be. What this was, however, I could not be sure. An uncertainty. Some unknown turning itself against me. I tried to shake the feeling and resumed battle mode. Ready for the black machine to enter my combat zone. But I was still unable to shift the obstinate uncertainty penetrating, deeper inside me. For now, the loyalty I held with the Snake grew dimmer. The allegiance I swore was now obscure and although I shunned its appearance, I knew I could not survive without its existence.

"No," I found myself suddenly repeating over and over until my clenched hands began to unfold. Something was wrong!

"Abort. Abort!" I now instinctively obeyed from whose command was not entirely clear as the growing fear of only more uncertainties unglued the weapon from my hands. It fell uneasily at my feet.

"Fool Louis. You Fool! Pick up the pike!"

When its reproach suddenly seized over me, it began to speak again. *"Does your folly come to extend itself against the whole of the empire? Pick up the pike, Louis. Pick it up! Retribution now lies at your feet. Your reprisal is at hand. Pick it up, Louis, Pick up the pike!"*

I tried to reply but my attempts were fruitless. My lips wanted to rebuke its slippery tongue, but I felt helpless. While I had only known the Snake to be deceptive and an offender to the moral Code of any true Civilization, it still had a hold on me. Submissively I obeyed. Bowing forward I picked up the pike.

Firmly I held the pike's long fuselage again. Adrenaline was firing on all cylinders, as the machine and its adversary grew closer. The silence that suddenly surrounded me was deafening. Reigning terror over me as I waited for my sovereign to decide.

At last the finality of its rule was delivered.

"Attack!"

Swiftly, the still sounds from the phalanxes of my body immediately responded. Drawing my weapon once more, I stepped onto the road without thought. My body was in control and its instinctive reactions would be tested. As I charged forward, the pike became the pilot of my flesh. A pilot that would lead me to my destination. When the Lincoln Mark V accelerated before the stretch, I felt an unquenchable thirst for blood. I waited for the other cars to pass before charging to the center of the road. Face-off! The machine and I would soon collide. Calculating my measured strides, I aligned the pike's deadly tip with my target. Labored breaths and blood pumping through me were the only sounds I heard when I lunged into the air. Then my missile-like body slammed onto the machine's long hood shielding all its eight, moving pistons beneath me. The pike and my outstretched body gliding along top the machine's glazed steel. While my eyes stayed open for one last moment before the pike's decisive strike shatters the windshield ahead. My victim just ahead, blind however, to the closing moments until I called out.

"Stop. Stop!"

The flesh of my prostrated body cried out as the cloudy appearance of the driver suddenly lifted.

"Stop!"

When suddenly the driver's outline was replaced by an unobstructed vision of the Snake. The one who designed this evil script. Although it had the power to awaken me, it left me powerless to change any script that it had written. The forces of its creation could not be swayed, and as a result its unyielding strength powered through me. I tried to drop the pike, but this only tightened my grip. The Snake had taken over.

"Stop!" I cried out in vain. "Stop this madness!"

I knew and understood the Snake's genius and the extent of its control over me. It had always been treacherous, but now I had witnessed this on a much grander scale. While now I saw the horror from the windshield I now stared into.

I tried but could do nothing to stop it when the strength of its objective came crashing through the car's windshield. Shattering glass all around me. Covering me and the driver. Then I watched in terror as my lover, Miss Tolemy, was immediately struck.

"Stop," I commanded the forces that possessed me.

The pike's cold steel unmercifully struck her while she begged and pleaded. Her anguish resonated throughout my being but still there was nothing I could do. I had to wait for the Snake to be satisfied before it allowed me to release my grip from the pike. Its task was now complete or so I thought at the time.

Slowly I opened my eyes. It seemed like they'd been closed for an eternity. With bloodied hands from the shattering glass, I began to quickly assess my unperceived dilemma but struggled to look beyond my outstretched arms to see. When suddenly the car sped up unexpectedly as I now used my freed hands to seize the hood's rear edge. There was now a new plight before me as the unpiloted foot of my lover accelerated in a frenzy until we were on the school lawn. My perilous limbs and torso swinging side to side, atop the machine's glazed steel. While I held onto the hood's rear edge, I ardently wanted to look at my lover one last time.

However, from my precarious position I could not see beyond the machine's steering wheel. I tried to twist my head around but it proved difficult when my body jostled from side to side. I kept trying, but the speed of the vehicle was unyielding.

"No!" I suddenly cried out. "For what have I ever done to you, while feeding on your lies? You always take from me, Snake!" My heartfelt anger continued to pour out as I thrashed about on the hood's warm steel.

"No, you bastard!"

I continued screaming until the machine's path suddenly became clear. Its climactic end near as at last I was able to see behind me.

Holding on for grim life, my bloodied hands sank deeper into the windshield's glassy bits, I was now fully aware of the catastrophe just ahead and quickly turned away.

Keeping my head low, I squeezed my eyes shut. My heart pounded faster in the impending seconds leading to impact. Then suddenly it struck.

The machine and all its impetus force crashed into the trunk of one, tall, formidable oak. The impact impelled my body forward and forced my grasp from the hood's rear edge; driving the top side of my head into the machine's steering wheel. Although my vision was diminishing, an instant spark of light ignited inside me. We were together this once more. A conclusion reassuring our place together as it felt time was now ending.

I remember... remember when sleep was merely a dream. Where her lips touched mine and her flesh joined with my own. I remember when our bodies lay motionless in bed, and hours drifted by.

My brief dream soon vanished, and I woke up with a gentle breeze whispering softly against the sweat streaming from my flesh. My eyes still shut.

The pounding pain from inside my head made me quickly realize this was not just another dream. And as I came to, I gradually became aware of the morbid scene around me. With arms outstretched my legs lay sprawled against the machine's warm steel. While my head and torso rested on the glassy dashboard beneath me.

The surreal atmosphere suddenly gave way to reality. For now the shallow breaths from my lover's own lips began to echo through the carnage around me. Desperately painful and cruel when next I would open my eyes once more. Facing an uninhabited passenger from which now my reclaimed vision could see a glassy surface beneath me smeared with my own sweat and blood. Slowly I began shifting my face against the shattered bits. Blood dripping from the pike's blunt end standing near me. Awakening me at once to the destruction my own hands created.

I continued to watch the blood drip down, the pike's deadly shaft, horrified by what I'd done. There would be no merciful conclusion for my beloved. Her breath lingered before me as I heard voices in the distance. Moving my aching body carefully through the broken bed of glass, I tried to look away from the gruesome scene but what good would that do? I knew that her waning breath alone would haunt me and fill my probing soul with fear. This is what the Snake wanted. To forever torment my heavy soul. To please itself through its perversion.

Yes, look away. Away. If only I could, I said to myself.

For the Snake's malign attraction to unholiness would only urge my eyes to absorb the bloodied pike and Miss Tolemy even more so. When next I began to raise my head from its side while I listened to her irregular, laden breaths between us. At last I could see over the steering wheel and quietly upon her.

Painfully I watched the slight opening of her lips as they drew short and quick gasps. Her head was tilted back, and hauntingly fixated on some unknown point outside. Blood spatter covered her face, clothing, and the car's interior from the collision and the pike's revenge. A pinhole Wound on her neck found a mist of blood escaping through her torn flesh. The pike's rounded, hollowed point striking its target with an absolute precision. Violently crushing my lover's trachea into her esophagus. An unforgivable act from the Snake who maliciously sharpened its instrument of death, taken the love it had bestowed, just as quickly as it'd been given.

Helplessly I cried out while gently placing my pierced hand from the sharp bits of glass on her cold face. The spray of blood from her neck now sprinkled onto my own hand. Then her eyes aligned with mine and she tried to speak out against this tragedy. Where now only death could offer its sole comfort. She struggled to breathe and her words grew more silent.

"Do not forget me my lover. Close your eyes my true love and never forget me."

"He Is In The Woodshop"

"That is far enough! An ambulance will arrive here shortly. Now stay back students. Stay back from that car at once!" Voices from outside my own theater of pain. As I now wanted to unleash this, agony from within. This wrath invading me. Exchanging it for revenge as my cold hand withdrew from her lifeless flesh. Its presence now my only solace as Moloch would call me again. Though understanding as well the voice of reason to at last abandon me. Now, revenge would be my ally.

"Louuuieee. Louis, stand up!" Its whisper spoke again. "Your nemesis is near. He is near, Louis."

"Voice, is that you? Are you at last summoning me?"

Yes Louis. It is me. Only now you must stand up. For he is close by. Winston is near!"

"Winston? Near..? Where? Where does this treacherous being now stand?"

"The woodshop. He is in the woodshop Louis, but you should already know that he always dwells in the woodshop."

"As you always dwell inside me?"

"Yes Louis, I am always by your side."

"But what happened then? What happened to our enemy that you vowed to eliminate? You weren't by my side then. Though after all, you are the Snake. Cunning in nature as you rule through your deception. What happened? What happened in the mere moments that led to

Miss Tolemy's demise? What? This is not what I wanted. You took my lover away from me. Why? What happened Snake?"

"What happened is you failed to love me. You loved her more and she became your sole obsession."

"So this is why you took my lover from me? Why should I even try to understand? Why?"

"Yes, why indeed. But now your true nemesis is not far and for this reason you must stand up. Stand up now Louis and take my hand once again!" "Yes, my enemy is not far. As he is always close by. I'll comply this one last time but don't expect me to understand your reason for taking away my love." I gave this more thought. "There never really is one last time with you is there?"

"No, I am a part of you don't you see. Now take my hand and correct what can be corrected. Take it Louis. Take my hand and stand up with me."

Suddenly a female voice on the outside cut into my conversation. But still I thought I was talking to Moloch, the Snake.

"Louis? Louis it's me. It's me Louis. Can you hear me?"

Yes, I can hear you as I listen and obey you always."

"Louis, who are you talking to? It's me Marie."

"Marie? Marie Antoinette? Now there was a voice I recognized from long ago. But I thought you had gone far away? Why are you here now? You must go away! Go away Marie and leave me now!"

"Who? Marie Antoinette? No, it's me, Marie Romano. I'm in the same history class as you but this car? I saw you on top of this car when it crashed into this tree. Are you alright? Who is that inside? Louis, who is that?"

"Marie Romano? Why do you call yourself that now? Never mind. Just get out of here. My task is not finished. Now leave!"

"What task? What has happened to you Louis, and this car? This black... Hang on... Yes, I know whose car this is. It's unmistakable. The Woodshop teacher. That's who this car belongs to but that is not Mr. Rumstitch inside. It is Miss Kapankee. The English teacher. Only now she looks... dead. She's not breathing! Only why are you on top of this car? What have you done? What have you done Louis!"

Dead and only too correct, I thought then immediately wondered about the name that had no meaning for me, Miss Kapankee? Who on Earth was she? And how had this stranger taken my lover's identity? Yes, a stranger.

Only what if this Marie Romano truly existed and Marie Antoinette was imagined? My heart sank, wondering if my Miss Tolemy ever existed at all. Was she another lie? A figment of my imagination?

"No Louis. You must stop this delusion. This madness you speak from. Marie Romano holds no secrets. No wealth of importance. She is the lie, Louis. For how long has Alexander the Great survived? Julius Caesar and your Miss Tolemy? The lie rests on those who fail to raise up its creed. The Napoleonic-Caesarism system. That is where the truth begins and where immortality begins to live."

"Marie, I told everyone to stay away from that car. Move back at once!"

The teacher's futile commands along with Marie's obstinate presence faded before me as the whole of my body now lifted from the black steel's carnage and the shadowy veil around me. Stepping away and into the glistening blue skies where a path of life for life would now command my next actions.

As I walked I obeyed in its silence and began to set my course back through the school's parking lot and to the woodshop. Towards Winston whose page from life I would now tear away from as quickly as he had torn from me.

While now the steadfast symmetry of my steps carried me through the chaotic mass of students and teachers in the parking lot as they scattered on sight of me. Though through my funneled vision, their faces looked blurred and any words that poured from their lips were inaudible. But their curiosities were short lived. Now their sole focus was on the bloodied carnage I had just removed myself from. Absorbed in this sinister curiosity, the mass quickly dwindled as I approached the school's posterior where the wood, auto, and metal shops were. However, I only sought the woodshop and its dweller.

Where now moments later I would find myself before an oversized gray metal door which did little to mute the buzzing sounds from the machinery within. I knew that Winston was on the other side cutting his wood as I stared back at the deep crimson letters marked "Woodshop." Idly waiting for the Snake's tongue to appear. However, failing to reason at the same time how it had just abandoned me once again.

Though paradoxically fearing its tongue was now indebted to me for the havoc the Snake created in my heart and for its deliberate treachery against me. I needed to be compensated as it was now obligated to satisfy my vengeance. Only I knew, I understood that I wasn't in any position to make demands. In the Snake's eyes, obedience was solely required of me and not the other way round.

I next placed my hands on the door's quivering handle and pushed it open. Quietly edging through the tight chasm I created, the door closed behind me.

There he stood. The man of wood, some thirty feet away, His spindly, skeletal hunched back faced me. He was oblivious to my covert presence as Moloch was preparing myself for him. As the rapid spinning blade of the table saw cut through another piece of wood. Silently I waited.

"Louis, Louis, here I am. To remind you where your obedience comes from. Now the instrument of execution lays neatly before you. The blade Louis. The spinning blade!"

Yes, the spinning blade, I thought. Where soon my vengeance will complete itself. From where its tongue will next guide me.

Buzz... then into the large box, more undesirable pieces of scrap. There use now questionable. While the more useful pieces Rumstitch neatly stacked beside him.

He would continue this repetitious task next to a large stack of more wood yet to be cut. All the while oblivious to his own imminent mortality. For Winston remained inside his world of wood with his oversized blade. Believing this could compensate through any and all physical and intellectual infirmities acquired throughout his own misguided intentions and from a life squandered.

"The spinning blade, Louis. The spinning blade...!"

Repeatedly, its tongue now, commanded. While my mind played out a strike where my enemy would fall unaware. An all-out blitz attack from which my actions would prove swift and absolute. The trinity of my strength would come from my mind, being, and own hands.

"Now Louis, You must do it now. Now!"

"Now Louis," I abruptly cried out at long last. Charging with longing, I strode toward him and throughout a space that seemingly stretched on forever. Now ominously reminiscent from a short time ago. Closing, closing, the gap between us was closing until I reached my clueless opponent. He caught sight of me over the nearly deafening buzz of the running blade. Revealing an alarming gaze of cold darkness even before death had a chance to strike. In an instant he understood the task I'd been given. An attack on right and wrong.

An offering without mercy. Without quarter.

I quickly smote both hands on my enemy's shoulders whose jutting skeletal blade's seemingly had their own sharpened edge. At once, I pushed Winston toward the table's blade, removing his stare away from me.

At first, his strength proved defenseless. He was utterly helpless against my own swift unsuspecting descent as I drove the whole of my reprisal against my victim's will to survive, but he became repellant. The weary, deformed, hunched back of my enemy offered an unexpected resistance to my own propelling force. I realized then his desire to live out another day. While Winston attempted to push away from the table's edge, his arms tried to gain leverage against my own strength. We struggled to overpower one another and he fought to erect himself against the weight of my own body. Struggling relentlessly, I continued to push downward against his own incessant will.

Soon the taxing impasse of our struggle would yield a more favorable outcome for me. Discovering my strength, once more, I eventually overcame the awkward humped extension on my enemy's rear torso. Driving Winston nearly atop the table's running blade, I used my left forearm, to thrust his shoulder blades down. Then used my right hand to push against the back of his outstretched neck. He used his rising strength to try to remove my grip, but it was no use. I still had the upper hand. Then suddenly his one hand slipped from the table's edge and perilously moved forward onto the table's surface. A sole cry from beneath me rang out before an immediate stream of blood followed. While his screams would continue as he looked at his now nearly fingerless hand.

Only his thumb remained.

Only his struggle to survive would stand unfazed against the whole of my prowess. With urgency I continued to push the outstretched neck of my foe toward the running blade. Positioning Winston's neck over the blade's vertical rotation so he could observe it from above. The blade remained unwavering however my own strength was diminishing. I knew I could not endure this struggle much longer and used all my force to push my victim closer to the cutting edge. I watched as a formidable breeze from the spinning blade hovered above Winston's hollowed eyes. Then I attempted to push him into the blade one more time. But the overly extended portion of his humped posterior became an obstacle. As he shifted awkwardly on his hump, my hand and wrist began to weaken. Finally, the last attempts from my wearying body gave way.

The rising momentum from my adversary sprung into survival mode, and he began to push back. Back and away from death's taunt. The strength of my forearm which was placed in the chasm of Winston's back, began to suddenly rise to my hand and wrist. I pushed back but the unforeseen force of my enemy now countered my every action. "Where are you?" I implored,

"Where are you?" I asked again. "Where is the strength of your tongue in this time of need? Our need."

Only its tongue was silent once more as the hunched back's strength increased and lifted me from behind. I had lost my stronghold, and now the leverage from my legs grew strained.

"Where?" I cried. "Where are you?!"

Then suddenly my prevailing strength completely collapsed before me. I was thrown off my adversary's hunched back and now Winston stumbled from the table's blade along with me. Fruitlessly I reached out to him with my legs stumbling behind me. Falling from an unexpected scenario, now Winston reeling over me. *"Stand up Louis,*

Stand up! Stand and finish our work. Our unfinished labors. Now stand up!"

Its selective tongue called out and once again I stood on proper footing, quickly realizing I was standing over a trail of bloody droplets from Winston's own four, severed Fingers, I began to follow his bloodied attempt to escape. Appreciating the urgency to swiftly subdue my prisoner at once, I started running toward him. Lowering my shoulder with each stride, like a football player, I tackled Winston from the most perfect angle and drove my shoulder into his exposed abdomen. Then I lifted his feet from the floor and dragged him to a nearby work bench. Slamming his body onto the table, we quickly found ourselves struggling as before, albeit without one rapidly spinning blade. While understanding that I could only hold onto him for a short period before fatigue set in again.

With my legs firmly planted, I used the weight of my extended body to Keep Winston's lower half pinned against the table's edge. Then began to briefly scan the table's surface for a suitable means of execution until I pushed him forward and over the table. Now pressing down on his head with one hand and using the other to feel along the bench for a tool as this was now my only means of vision. For now my focus was strictly on Winston who was still struggling against me while my other hand hovered over the table's uneven surface. When at last that freed hand would prove itself a worthy peripheral aid when it seized onto an unmoving, solid, metal object at the table's edge. One jawed bench vice that was firmly bolted down.

A jawed vice? What could I do with that? I cannot pick it up and strike him squarely over his head? Though I could try, I thought in my hastened urgency. Only I quickly surveyed the idea before abandoning any such momentary lapse of flawed reasoning. A deliberate contribution to delay my actions from the Snake no doubt.

While I continued to push against my adversary, I thought about how one action could beget another. How my lapse in thinking was used as an advantage by my enemy. Now Winston used the opportunity to fight for his very survival. He nearly threw me off his backside. Rising one last time from death's reprisal, he stood upright alongside me. I removed my scavenging hand from the vice and now placed both hands on his head in a dire attempt to push his head back down on the splintered table. Then suddenly I heard a burning cry. His last desperate hope for escape. Now through a series of attempts to throw me off his torso, Winston violently jerked up and back, but this only proved pointless in any bid to remove me. For my legs and footing remained steadfast to the floor. My strength drawing from its proper source now attached to his weakening hopes. Winston's fate was nearly complete as my sight suddenly retrieved its peripheral advantage once more. All I had to do was keep him and quickly find a proper implement to finish him off. Although we stood nearly upright my left forearm remained on Winston's upper back while both hands pressed on his resisting head and outstretched neck. From this vertical angle I could scan the table's surface once more. My eyes veered back and forth over the same viced jaw and there it was. The implement's small appearance. I must have overlooked ten times over through my hastened pursuit. Lying directly above Winston the tool looked meager, and easy to miss. Though its length would be easy to maneuver. Its accuracy deadly. It was lying there as if it knew its assignment, it's one function to carry out.

Only now our near vertical stance made it impossible to reach this simple tool. As my thoughts continued inside this ceaseless urgency, I knew I needed to coordinate my last prevailing strike before its final conclusion. Immediately I used the remaining strength I had. Drawing myself slightly away from my Victim, I then erected the length of my torso and shoulders in cobra like fashion. Priming myself toward my antagonist, I kept my feet firmly planted on the floor and retracted my upper body. I briefly removed my hand and arm away from Winston to spring forward at his hunched back. My left forearm struck his backside while my hand attached to his head, and neck as before. The compelling momentum drove Winston's face into the table's surface. When he cried from beneath me, I reached out and snatched the dormant implement above his head.

The oblong wood handle fit neatly inside my warm palm as I held the pointed awl. Brandishing the slender shafted point close to his neck and above his face: I wanted him to take a good look at my weapon. With repeating cries for help, he tried desperately to remove himself from me.

However, soon I would hear his last desperate cry. From a forty-five-degree angle I swiftly wielded the small authoritative weapon at Winston. His head and shoulders inclined back from my aim as the instrument's sharpened shank quickly found an eye socket. The pointed awl drove itself upwards, passed a sinking eyeball and into his skull's cavity. Only the sounds of his gasp was heard from under my final task. An immediate climax, to which I promptly released myself from. His lone struggle was over. Now we staggered away from one another.

I stood still and watched Rumstitch in the most frenzied state. His cries continued though without a voice. Only moans and grunts now uttered from his speech. The awl still protruded from his collapsed eye. His legs and feet suddenly stumbled beneath him while his arms oddly raised and stretched before he removed the bloodied shank. Quickly pulling its shaft through a now wounded eye and socket. Next, I shadowed my enemy from a seemingly endless blind circle of confusion. I would ensure that he took his last breath before me. Winston no longer seemed interested in Freedom outside his beloved woodshop, but he realized I was still present. For he suddenly and unexpectedly lunged toward my encircling taunts. His Frankenstein stagger and his arms stretched out before him, as he searched for me. We encircled one another until I abruptly found myself precariously opposite his now vengeful pursuit. He lunged again and pinned me to the table's edge and took a firm hold of my neck, proving his remaining fingers were a fierce foe. His force pushed me back and I felt his waning breath heavy against my skin, as I struggled to breath. I began to cough in search for another swallow of air, but his remaining six fingers continued their asphyxiating revenge. However, this was cut short. Soon Winston's last will to survive would meet its final climax. I could feel the strength of his fingers relaxing around my throat and his breath became more laden and rapid until it lessened, then finally left him entirely. His body fell onto mine, and his now motionless six fingers rested on my strained neck. One eye stared into my own, spreading disdain throughout my flesh. I quickly threw his cadaverous hunched back off me. Leaving his mortal refuse lying on the table's surface to never look back.

Only now any hope of a quick exit from the woodshop, and my host vanished. The strength in my legs had departed without warning and my limbs felt like they were detaching themselves from the rest of my body. But I somehow made it to the door's exit. Reaching out. Reaching toward her. My Miss Tolemy. Reaching, reaching only to grow fainter. Weaker as she grew darker. Forever. Forever in darkness, her name would spill from my lips: "Miss Tolemy...Miss Tolemy!"

"Water"

Yes. I remember now. I remember its deceptive, navigating tongue. Only giving to take back at will. Though most of all I remember her.

"Mr. Ney. Can you hear me? Can you hear me, Louis Ney?"

Voices. Again. No wait... a different voice. When have you addressed me by any other name than Louis? No, only Louis, I thought. This voice was much gentler than the Snake's voice. It was softer.

"Miss Tolemy...? Miss Tolemy is that you?"

"Miss Tolemy? No Louis, it's your nurse. Nurse Monroe, You have been asleep for a while now. Why don't you try to open those eyes so you can see me?" Yes, I uttered quietly within, before I spoke to her with my eyes open. "Nurse?"

"Yes, I am your nurse. Can you see me now?"

"I can," I began as I immediately observed the leather straps binding my limbs tightly onto some cold bed. There was another strap across my torso. The only furnishing in this room, where seemingly the light never leaves, was this lone, raised bed that I was adhered to.

"But why?" I asked, "Why have you bound me against a bed where the cold always pervades me?"

"You are at the jail. Inside the jail's psychiatric ward."

"Psychiatric ward?"

"Yes Louis." The nurse continued. "I was told you became quite upset and violent yesterday once the local police woke you. Don't you remember? The police found you asleep over at the high school. Inside the woodshop lying near the door. Do you remember?"

"Remember? Remember what? Her? Miss Tolemy?"

"Who is this Miss Tolemy you keep on your tongue? At any rate, as I was just saying they I mean the police found you fast asleep over at the high school, though as indicated by our staff, you are perfectly fine, except..."

"Except what? What nurse?" I interjected. "Blood. The jail staff below us had to wash a lot of blood off you. But the woodshop Louis. Can you remember anything about the woodshop?"

"The woodshop," I began reflecting. "Yes Louis. The woodshop over at the high school."

"Yes, I remember. Where Winston offered himself through his own treachery against me and the state."

"Hmmm, alright then. Do you need anything? Water or are you hungry? The doctor should be here shortly."

"What do you think I need? These straps nurse. Remove these straps!"

"Good afternoon Eva. I see our new patient is wide awake now."

"Yes doctor. He was just saying that he would like the straps removed."

"That will come soon enough," the doctor said, speaking directly over me. "I am Doctor Truman. The jail psychiatrist."

"Psychiatrist?"

"Yes. I am the psychiatrist here at the jail."

"Only why? Why do you want to examine me?" I quickly surmised as much.

"Just precautions Mr. Ney, Only precautions. Though it has been decided that you will be transferred to the state facility. That is the state psychiatric hospital where they have better means to treat you and evaluate your condition!"

"Condition? And just what is my condition?"

"That is what we need to find out, but I would like to ask you..." He stared at me before speaking again. "Did you...I mean were your intentions to...? Well, never mind. Never mind Mr. Ney. Now the ambulance will be picking you up sometime tomorrow morning and more than likely you'll be strapped down to a gurney, however you should remain unstrapped once at the hospital. Just follow their rules and you should be fine. Do you have any questions for me or Nurse Monroe?"

"Water... I need water!"

"Nurse Monroe will give you water. Okay then, I will see you in the morning."

"Good day nurse," he concluded.

"Good day doctor." I watched as her eyes followed him out.

"Here you are Louis. Raise your head up. Now how was that? Some more?"

"Water." I murmured through my now wet lips. Sleep suddenly found me once again. Her soft skin reaching gently behind my neck. Yes, here I am. Here I am dream.

"Dr. Josef Menjele"

"I can hear you Louis as I am here with you. Beside you Louis. You. Granting every touch, every taste and desire you wish for. From me Louis. Yes, only me. Miss Tolemy. I am your Miss Tolemy. I am she. Thus, listen and hear, hear me, Louis. Only me." "Louis? Louis the doctor would like to see you now. Louis. Wake up! Wake up now. Wake up!"

"No. Leave me and my dream. Go away from me!"

"Wake up Louis! Wake up. Wake up from your dream now. Wake up!"

Suddenly I woke up. Where there were no shackles binding me against my will. The bright light had been removed, albeit a cold bed was still beneath me.

"The doctor, and I would like to see you." She spoke from her glossy red lips. Only who was this bold, fair skinned creature who now talked over me?

"That's it Louis, Now come with me. Come and follow me. Come."

In my groggy state I followed my strange goddess, and found comfort watching her buoyant ass and hips. A dream? I wondered. Perhaps, but who is she and where am I now?

She led me to a room where I was greeted by another strange face. He sat behind an overly scratched and battered desk which was disheveled with scattered papers. As my mysterious enchantress guided me toward him, I noticed the temperature of the room. It was seemingly colder than the one I just left, and its unwelcoming chill immediately ran through me. My legs felt weak from the prolonged sleep I had at last come out of.

"Please sit down Louis or is it Lou?"

"Louis," I bluntly said as I sat before the middle-aged man who dressed older than his apparent age. His black suit and shirt looked strangely outdated, and I wondered if his father had passed them down to him, along with the white tie he donned. His overall attire looked odd with his shorter military cut hair style. While he continued to talk through his excessive smile, I found myself staring at the distinctive gap between his two upper front teeth.

"Then Louis it is. Well then, do you know where you are?" I continued to stare at his smile while he answered on my behalf.

"This is the Eden State Psychiatric Hospital near New Berlin. I will be your examining psychiatrist during your stay with us."

"Examining? My stay?" I repeated aloud while starting to feel a restless annoyance with the peculiar figure before me.

"Yes Louis, I am here to determine your full understanding of the current charges brought against you. The courts have chosen me as your doctor."

"My doctor? Doctor who?" I asked as I looked around his office. It didn't look like a typical doctor's office. Other than two filing cabinets, a desk and chairs, the room was barren. There were no degrees or family photos, displayed on his desk or on the walls. Was this strange man even a doctor?

"Who...? But you know me. My name. My mission."

"Josef Menjele. Doctor Josef Menjele," he said with a crooked smile as he rubbed his clean-shaven chin thoughtfully. Suddenly a second chill ran up my spine.

"Dr. Josef Menjele?"

"Yes Louis. That is my name. From our beginning until now... Josef Menjele."

"And I believe you have already met our head nurse, Miss Josephine. She will also be sitting with us today."

"Josephine," I uttered, turning my head away from the doctor to look at the gentle creature who now sat next to me.

"Now Louis," he continued while my eyes remained unmoved from Josephine. Her soot black hair suited her warm, fair skin. Who was she? My dream? The doctor's voice reached out to me again, "as I mentioned, you are here for us to assess, and determine your competency to stand trial if that's the path you and your lawyer take. That is, your ability to comprehend the charges and to see if you can adequately participate in your own defense." The doctor slowly leaned forward, crossing his arms at the desk's edge. "Do you believe you have this understanding or perhaps..."

"Or what doctor?" I asked, finally looking at him once more.

"Well, this report from jail suggests you may be experiencing hallucinations. It appears that you have a fixation with Napoleon and Caesar. Perhaps hearing voices which may undermine your ability to fully comprehend what you are being charged with."

"Do you understand what you are charged with?" The doctor unfolded his arms, grabbed a notebook and pen near him; ready to transcribe my every word.

"My accusers know. That is, they think they know. Now they have convinced themselves that I murdered two people. When in fact one was a mere accident of love while the other was only a suitable conclusion to his own treachery. It was him. He committed these crimes, not me."

"So what you are telling me is that you have not deliberately committed these two alleged murders?" the doctor asked, stopping his pen momentarily.

"I certainly did not! For it was deemed from his own desires to forfeit his very flesh when he decided upon what was not his to take. His own intentional betrayal is what decided his fate. There were consequences for his deliberate actions. I simply reacted."

"His deliberate actions, Louis? Hmmm...This shop teacher and what he allegedly took from you?"

"Yes, Winston." I replied.

"But this, "reaction" of yours. Could this not be considered vengeance on your part?"

"Yes, but not my own. Certainly not!"

"Then whose? Who carried out this crime where two people are now dead? Was there someone else with you? Who Louis? Who was there with you?"

"It," I suddenly confessed. "Yes, someone or something was with me. Though 'It' is always with me. It and its voice. Alongside its needs for both state and empire as Napoleon-Caesar would have willed. The Voice still dwells within me, inside me, but I don't think you would understand. For you cannot hear it. Its voice. Its living voice."

"How can I hear Louis if you do not try and make me understand? Explain to me what you hear so I can hear also. To help you. You need to talk to me Louis. Speak to me."

"Yes, speak to me Louis." Its cold smile began to announce itself once more. *"For we are both under the same laws that have brought us together. I have contributed greatly, through countless hours of conducting experiments. Performing acts that the law orders us to carry out. Only now you have created a path of betrayal between us. Abandoning the unconditional love I have for you. You need to come back to me. Come back and adhere to my counsel once again. It is only a small thing I ask of you. You need to draw yourself back to me. Renounce the very betrayal between us and return to me. Restore your obedience to me. Come back Louis. Return to me once more. Come back!"*

"Louis, what is it? You hear something don't you? Something or someone that I can't hear. What Louis? What is it you now hear?"

Suddenly, I seemed to awaken again. "Everything yet nothing at all. But its fruitless tongue dwells near."

"Near? Inside you?"

"Yes doctor. Inside where it has always been. It has never left me. Do you understand this? How it navigates its tongue inside both good and evil. Could you ever really know? Or precisely grasp its meaning through your textbooks and invasive psychological incisions that you perform on others like me? How can you know? How could you know? How Doctor?"

"You now ask me how I could know?" His gaping smile disappeared. "Nurse, could you please leave us alone?"

"Yes doctor, is there anything wrong?"

"On the contrary nurse, everything is just fine. I know you are aware of doctor/patient confidentiality." "But of course doctor." She immediately withdrew herself and his smile returned.

"You underestimate me Louis," he said, though now from a more austere likeness. "Underestimate my abilities as a doctor. My own meticulous qualities. I serve under no 'Hippocratic oath' which merely demonstrates one's conservative methods. No Louis, my methods are much more thorough than that. More visionary and complex in their response. A response that enables a genuine and ideal design to any one individual, or class of individuals. Where perfection is only sought out. Only perfection, Louis. You see, I do understand. I understand and I know you."

And from these words I silently freed myself from him. Only somehow I knew him as but how did I know him? From a past which wanted me to remember?

Days soon turned to weeks inside a hospital that only ensured my continuous madness.

"Take this Louis. It's good for you. Take it now." She would speak, though knowing it wasn't her will, but his own. The doctor's whose peculiar placement inside these walls came from another time. In a groggy stupor I would wait for him to reveal himself to me.

Now I could only watch as she gracefully walked about the hospital's corridors. Glancing subtly as she passed by. I decided that I needed to keep her away from me until the time was right for the two of us. Until I could remember my own past, which included the doctor. Then she would draw her bosom closer to me. Leaving no doubt of her love once again. Somehow this creature had resurrected and come back to me. Yet it also seemed that her presence never left me. Miss Tolemy's presence.

To bide time while I thought more clearly about my past, I decided to fulfill my immediate needs, with one, tiny, slut, whore called Geneva. Whose depressive, social anxiety outbursts only fueled her wishes for more clandestine meetings. With her I would satisfy physical needs and nothing more.

While now my only true obsession was with the doctor's words: "I know you." These three words would continue to haunt me as the days passed by within these walls. Although the obsession could have stemmed from the methodic sedation under the doctor's ruling hand as well. However, one day its voice would briefly reappear through a clear photographic memory which would tell all.

"Louuuieee... Louis, it's me. Your sole counsel. He is now your lone enemy. Whose smile sits across from you. Him along with his crooked ways. Only remember one thing. Remember me!"

"Wake-up... wake-up!" I ordered myself aloud.

Within an hour I was able to retrieve that one lost portion of memory, from long ago, along with my oppressor. Through our regular inquisitions, my memory that was buried deep inside would at last give root. While facing him once more I would unveil my recent discoveries.

"And how do you feel today, Louis? You look a bit tired. Perhaps you are not getting enough sleep?" To which I merely stared back.

"Now where did we leave off the last time we met? Ahhh yes, I remember now. Those two brutal murders at your high school. Do you still refuse to admit any guilt or are you ready to rethink your response?"

"Well Louis? Are you going to just sit there with no declaration of any wrongdoing? Well, are you? Are you guilty?"

"You are him!" I blurted out. "You are Death!" I glared back from across his desk when suddenly his lost image from long ago reappeared.

"No Louis. I am not who you think I am. I am not it! You are mistaken." His tone suddenly became calm, which strangely alarmed me even more.

"On the contrary, you are quite mistaken. Because I have given life. Pursuing its perfect embodiment. Granted to those deemed worthy and more acceptable."

"I give life!"

No, no it's a lie! I spoke back against him.

"I remember now. A camp where my mother, father, and I were forced into. I also recall a name that was spoken of inside the camp. A name where the human tragedy was nothing short of diabolical proportions. A camp where you governed while playing a kind of demigod to thousands under your command. Their fate was under your control. You were an overseer of life and death and you commended the latter many more times over."

"Hmmm.... Louis, I am trying to understand this other side of you. Perhaps you've been spending too much time in the showers with that bitch, Geneva."

"Don't you mean your poisonous showers? Your chambers of death that are marked by a peculiar sign, laid out within a set of plain lines moving inside two different directions. One from vertical to horizontal then back to vertical. The other from horizontal to vertical then horizontal once more. A strange and twisted design. Symbolic for its declaration and dedication to hatred of those who are judged 'unfit' in the eyes of those who believe in their pseudo superiority."

"Now you chatter as if you are an imbecile. Vertical to horizontal then back to vertical. What strange words you speak, Louis. But then again for a moment I forgot where you reside presently."

"Then I shall explain, more clearly for your benefit and yours alone."

"Please do. Sort out this distorted illusion. This madness I am being accused of."

"Yes, then I shall proceed. From your own distorted belief marked by a black symbol on a red and white motif. It is a flag saluted by oppressors who like yourself believe that life solely matters to those who are regarded more "proper" and appropriately more "suitable." It is from these beliefs your death chambers emerge marked by their black symbol of hate."

"But I gave you life. I spared you from inevitable death! Do you not remember this?"

Yes, but not my mother and father.

You sent him into the poisonous chambers right away, while you let my mother live. That is, on your conditions and since she was cast from your own stock, you thought you showed her mercy. But you did not. The hard labor was agonizing. You tortured her because she loved someone who was not of your own bloodline. Eventually, you saw to her slow death. After you killed both my parents I viewed my own life from a very precarious circumstance. I was a young child without adult skills to keep me alive. Each hour of the day and night I lived in constant fear with no mother or father nearby. However, throughout these fears a miraculous mercy materialized. Though unsuspecting at first from its outer sheep's clothing, I quickly realized its own emerging evil and the infernal role it played inside the camp."

"For it was you one day who took me away from the barracks and brought me into your home. Where there was no pain and suffering like that which surrounded it. Only it was here I discovered who you were. Your leading role inside the cleansing you watched over."

"Yes, you commandant. Doctor Josef Menjele! I watched you as well. I watched as you nonchalantly brushed ashes from your unsullied uniform. When I polished the ash off your boots, I knew it came from the unceasing burning ovens. You doctor. You in the name of diabolical hate."

"And all this you thought up yourself? This phantom apparition. Please go on. I'm curious to hear more from this strange Voice you continue to uncover."

"Only this is no flawed memory. You quickly placed me with a small child who I initially thought was like myself. But through your corrupted lens I had half-bred status, and was unlike this other child who belonged to a master race. This child belonged to you, and as I played with him the ovens burned. Day and night they burned and the rising ashes darkened the sun."

"Only you could not stop with just my mother and father. No, it was your necessity, your essential need to continue your personal onslaught. While somehow I believed I was saved from your daily atrocities that surrounded me inside your camp. But I soon realized that I was just some toy for your only son. A toy until I wasn't, anymore. Only now I remember. I remember everything. Your unsettling presence has brought back what I thought was lost. A reminiscence of the clear evil you oversaw and acted upon, you could not even leave one living soul untouched that was deficient in your eyes. And while others were ruthlessly slaughtered your descent upon me was more subtle. More gentle, I dare say, in your experimentations. Once a week you would turn your thoughts, your logic toward me, and I would receive such reasoning: A 'cure' you would claim. One that would almost always end in death for others. Though if death did not occur straight away, your victims suffered some form of paralysis or other physical deformity which guaranteed their trip to the ovens anyway. The most horrific experiment I witnessed was the slower death where little by little a man's brain gradually rotted away from him."

"And still you are here. Before my very eyes." he said leaning closer. His stare resolute. "You are strong as two assassinations prove on your part. Cunning as well. You seem deceitfully intelligent while you carry on this chatter. But I must admit that I'm surprisingly amused to hear your story through. Now please if you will. Please...I insist!"

"Yes, you are absolutely correct doctor." I proceeded once again. "I did survive your weekly injections, pumping tainted fluid inside my veins. You so zealously wanted an outcome which you could not achieve through me. My skin didn't change, my hair remained dark and my eyes didn't miraculously turn blue. This bothered you, and I often overheard you complaining: 'But our child needs a proper playmate, you would so ardently confide in your wife. One whose skin is purer, whose hair is fairer, and whose eyes shine brighter.'"

"Only this would not take place from the trial and error you so passionately performed on those like me. What's more, if it wasn't for our liberation I am certain, I would have perished. Sooner rather than later."

"This is all very interesting Louis, however now I have grown weary from listening to your gibberish about burning ovens and your tainted injections. Even so, I believe you are not finished with me yet. Please conclude what you began but remember that your words will not be the last from this script!"

"I know my words to be true," I continued. "You used a myriad of oppressive methods. Methods that aligned with your genuine madness. Your approaches were so evil I suppressed these memories while I was growing up. From your ever satiable diabolical need to your outright slaughter of innocent people. As an implorable means of self suppression, I ran from these memories with a seemingly deliberate and calculating subconscious."

"Now I remember the long awaited liberation from your camp. Only your hand would continue to hold tightly with mine as the creation thereafter began. Moloch, whose voice dwells with me now. But freedom did land throughout Europe and beyond and my new set of parents brought me across the ocean to another world. A land with a new beginning. One which fate allowed us to reunite."

"So doctor? Commandant! How is your son, you bastard?"

"Indeed Louis... Indeed," was his lone reply. His smile looked colder than before. I took this as an admission of guilt.

I considered my ultimate charge against him. One I could deliver to the monster who aligned himself against humanity. I would do this for all humanity who had suffered at his hands, I slowly next raised my left forearm then sliding back my sleeve, which covered my tattoo. I took my time rolling it up as I wanted my accusations to be known clearly and from whom.

An accusation which spoke for my mother and father; their mothers and fathers and sons, and daughters; grandsons and granddaughters, nieces and nephews and cousins...

"Why, you are one of them," he said, when at last I finished raising my marked forearm for his vigil eyes to inspect. "No doubt in my mind Louis, you are one of them."

He spoke with callous sarcasm as he read the six numbers tattooed on my flesh. Digits that were also etched into my inner being. My very soul! At a glance he knew perfectly well what those six numbers, tattooed neatly along the inside of my forearm represented. It was personal. It was his own internal justice created by his own hands.

"Yes doctor so I am one of them. One whose lives you marked forever," I said, lowering my arm from his glare.

"Is that all Louis? Are you finished with your yakety yak about this and about that? You are all consumed by your chatter. Though is this not a distinction you all possess?"

"Now let me tell you something!" His gaped tooth retort commenced. "Something perhaps your simple understanding cannot grasp There are other fragments you fail to recognize! Circumstances which elude those who are like you, who are not inherited from an accepted model of a solely pure and unblemished foundation. You see progress is founded within a society only when society allows itself to become authentic. Filtering all contamination that impedes its progress. It's Esprit de Corps. Where from an entity not seen since the beginning of mankind."

"Since the beginning of time doctor? Should I now believe that you have such intimate knowledge from the beginning? Though, certainly you are correct. I do not stand by those ideals and principles you hold. I am nothing like you. Created from some unholy seed. Sinister in its origin."

"Hmmm......so now you want me to believe your very own virtuous good? You deceive yourself with self-righteous chatter, while maintaining a kind of romanticized image from the blood that now stains your very hands."

"And suddenly I began to ponder. Reflect while my hands were stained with the blood of not one but two lives. Is not one too many...?"

"Yes Louis, you are everything like me."

"No... no!" My thoughts started to race. "I am nothing like you! You, along with the crippled principles you abide by. No... nothing!"

"Only why Louis? Why do you refuse this charge brought against us? One we share together? Why...?"

"You doctor are bred from another," I continued. "Another source! You are the original creator of death while I am only a fragment of your being. But I must take leave from you again and from the smoldering stench you always offer."

"Leave?"

"Yes, I must leave and go back to the cold room where only my dreams can comfort me," I replied, before a sudden lull washed over me. Drawing itself closer as the entity coiled itself inside my flesh. But when it started to speak, its apparition grew present.

"*You cannot escape from me. We have not finished what we set about.*"

"What I set about?"

"*Yes Louis, but what we set about. To which only we can accomplish. You must listen. Listen as before. Through me you shall act once more.*"

"Once more? As before? Before when?"

"*Before now Louis. Now! Don't you remember?*"

"Yes, I should think so. As before now seems more noteworthy from the others."

"*Yes Louis. You remember. You remember Winston's turmoil brought on by his own selfish cause.*

But I am here now, Louis, to tell you that your work is not finished!"

"Finished?"

"*Yes Louis. Your work is incomplete. You cannot begin until you finish what's at hand.*"

"And what is that? What? I have grown tired of the unfinished, incomplete work you present to me."

"*No, you must never tire from an incomplete task. Where any reoccurring state must repeat itself through its work from your own hands. Conditioning the present time from that of its previous time, where any certain ending never truly exists.*"

"*Your work is not complete Louis. Are you listening to me?!*"

"Yes, I hear you! Day and night it's only you I hear. Breeding lies while conveniently circumventing each truth with another lie."

"Yes, I can hear you... I can hear you!"

"Oh, how I used to need you and you alone. Like a woman one bonds with. Penetrating first at the surface then deeper, until you find yourself inside a dream of only repeated delusions, along her ceaseless uncertainties that never allow for any true commitment."

"Yes, you are all that and so much more!"

"Empty gibberish Louis. You babble on about everything but nothing at all. Can you still not see?"

"The man of wood," I swallowed aloud in pause.

"Yes, the man of wood."

"My mother. My father," I continued again, halting briefly.

"Yes Louis, your mother, your father, and brothers, and sisters. You need to act on their behalf: for their labors that remain unfinished."

"How? How should this come to be? Dear God how? I'm afraid of the outcome of what lies ever so dormant inside me. Afraid!" *"Oh no, you mustn't be afraid, but overcome any such fear until your labors reach their inevitable conclusion."* "Mother and Father," I repeated. "Mother and Father." "Then how? If I have been chosen again, how should I complete such labors?"

"Cut it out! You must cut it out!" It hissed while recoiling itself from the horror of its own command. *"You must cut it from you. Its rule from out of you. From its bowels of your inner depths. Wound its sovereignty which holds power over you. Cut it out, Louis. Cut it out!"*

"Cut it out?" I reflected, through parched lips. Suddenly its apparition departed, inserting itself inside me once more. Then I heard the doctor speak.

"What do you see?" he asked.

"You stare through your own words though I cannot hear or understand. It's as if some momentary trance suddenly prevailed over you."

"But I can see you doctor, and I can understand you as well. You take souls with bitter poison that permeates the flesh of those like me. But now the poison must be cut out. Your poison, doctor. Your soul!"

"Well then, I can see you have come back, Louis."

"Yes doctor, I have come back! I've come back to the cancer lying near me. It's close by." When from that moment I would behold its light once more. Readjusting my eyes as a narrow band of sunlight streamed through the window and illuminated an object on the doctor's desk. It was a polished nickel, silver, handle lying remotely on the rearmost edge. On closer inspection I realized it was a scalpel. The precision, 2 inch cutting blade rested between our still bodies, unmoved as if we were awaiting a storm. By the startled look in the doctor's eyes, I could tell he had evaluated the situation and was considering his next move.

"Cut it out. Now Louis! Move and cut it out now!"

I quickly stood up and grabbed the scalpel from the desk. Then waited for the Snake's command to carry out this sacrificial execution.

"Cut it out Louis. Cut it out!"

Suddenly a familiar scene played out in my mind. My body now stood directly over his, while brandishing the blade above his haunting gaze. I pursued my next thoughts and actions while I paradoxically pleaded for his unwarranted mercy. A quarter on his behalf though undeserving.

"No... no!" I cried out. "Not this time, Not again!"

Only I knew the Snake's will was overpowering my own as I clutched the doctor's neck. Squeezing tightly with my left hand, I used my forearm to push his chest back. All the while, the terrified doctor glared at the scalpel in my right hand. The angel of death now inundated by his own fears. Pushing, pushing, pushing back against his cries from below, I pushed until his head and neck could reach back no more.

"Cut it out Louis. Cut it out! Do not wait. Do not hesitate. You must cut it out now! Now Louis... Cut it out now!"

"No! No dear God, no Louis... no!" the doctor cried, though his attempts to struggle against me were futile. Holding the scalpel's cutting edge closer to his face, I began to wave the point of the blade from one eye socket to the next. When suddenly I remembered the six numbers burned inside my flesh. I then pressed harder on his throat, wanting to squeeze the life out of him.

"No Louis!" he mouthed through choked words.

"Now Louis. Now!"

"Yes, now I must. Now and forever!" I cried as I pressed the instrument against my foe's lips.

"Drop the blade, Louis. Drop the blade!" he murmured through his clenched lips as I continued to strangle him. His chest rose and fell as he tried to capture air. "Dear God, Louis.

Drop the blade!"

I would become besieged by the doctor's echoing message: "Drop the Blade." However, the Snake's imploring command to cut it out would also continue. Moloch had always beseeched me to do its dirty work, but now its requests would become more urgent. And its desperate need for air would only grow stronger.

The Snake's tongue could only hold out for so long. While I waited and waited…And then strike!

"I Remember"

Cold... I feel cold again. Cold through its cruel temperament coiling itself inside me... Yes... cold again, This coldness seems to always lie beside me.

I now remembered what happened before this cruel unwelcoming coldness found its way into my bones again. I had waited for the advent of its ascent while the steel blade remained attached to my flesh. I could feel the silent cries from within. Though from a sphere I could not recognize at the time. A surrealism I could not properly address, so I waited. Patiently awaiting its approach. Its final arrival!

Only now I felt bound once again. Bound from a time where my limbs lay still. Where any movement was restricted from the cold bed I once laid upon. Where even the opening of my eyes seemed impossible. Would my eyes now remain forever closed? Would my wrists remain without movement? My ankles too? I knew one thing: my capacity to hear would never waver.

Yes, now I remember...

When she once came into me, alongside the emerging stillness of its rise with its words, "Cut it out... Cut it out!" It would repeat these words until it spoke no more. All the while brandishing the blade against the lips of my foe. Waiting...

Then soon its inevitable need for more air drew itself out from the dark abyss. The cell of its evil black pit. Casting the soul of its belly from below as it recklessly implored its words upon me.

I remember... Her silent touch. Her lingering fragrance. Her permeating breath. This I remember.

From a time when its flesh was torn from it's seed. Ripped from its roots and cries from inside.

To never again abide alongside me. This I can remember...

Her loyal obedience to and only to me as she gave longing relief to my shackled ankles and wrists, which were bound every moment. She had given me relief each day when I was placed in yet another cold room that invaded my soul. Her maternal presence stayed close and allowed me to unconditionally surrender to her love. From the warmth of her palms and fingertips she begins. Slowly and alluringly she presses her body down on me, her lover. Our lips touch...

Yes, as it was now and before and from the beginning. This I remember.

"Good morning, Nurse Josephine." "Good morning, Doctor Fleming."

"And how is our patient feeling today?"

"He is quiet now. Not a stir. Still, I can only wonder what became of him yesterday. When I heard all that screaming and commotion inside your office, I quickly ran to see... why he had you by the throat before doing the most unthinkable..."

"I can tell you plainly why nurse. He is mad. Mad as all can be. Why his own delirium places him inside the very core of the German Holocaust; within the confines of some fictitious camp. He has even gone as far as carving a set of numbers along his forearm to further convince himself."

"I have seen those numbers myself. Though they hardly appear self-inflicted."

"Excuse me, nurse? It is my business to know these things. My duty to uncover mere fantasy from truth from every manic psychotic that passes through these hospital doors."

"Yes doctor, but if I may?"

"What nurse? If you may what?"

"I was only going to remark on the way he called you out. By another name. A Josef Menjele, I believe he called you."

"Yes, more delusion from an infinite pool of delusions. It's another case on point of how far he really is from reality."

"However, these displays of intolerable behavior can and will not be accepted at this hospital. Restraints and a good dose of medicine. That's our number one cure, nurse."

"Yes, perhaps, doctor. At any rate, I loosened his straps just before you arrived to keep his circulation moving."

"That's fine nurse. Just make sure you tighten those straps back as they were. We wouldn't want another episode after what happened yesterday."

"Yes, but of course doctor. Only, are these straps still necessary?"

"Absolutely necessary! Why, you saw it yourself. Mr. Ney has earned himself this spot for the time being, and while he may have secured his permanent stay with us, he won't be acting out any longer if I have anything to say about it. Now only his dreams alone can take him away from this place."

"Yes, those dreams doctor. They appear so dark at times."

"Yes, but I don't think even 'dark' can define that mania he experiences inside those dreams he tries to hold onto."

"Louieee... Do you hear me? Can you hear me?!"

"Again doctor. Look again, he murmurs so."

"Yes, nurse, I can see that. It's the medicine that's taking him deeper." The doctor crinkled his nose. "Although he could use a proper bath. His odor is becoming more pungent than ever."

"Right away, but do you mean a…?"

"A sponge bath nurse. Only a sponge bath. This one's overwhelming odor won't excuse him from this room yet!"

"I'll fill a basin at once."

"Good, then I'll leave you to that task and I will check on our patient later. Good day, nurse!"

"Louis? Can you hear me? Hear me Louis! It is me again. You and me. Alone, alongside your dreams once more. Reigning over you, over you like the deep sleep which now afflicts you. Louis? Can you hear me?"

Whispers speaking to me? Whispers that touch my ears, while my eyes stay closed and my speech is silent.

I remembered I held a blade from a moment, horrific in its cries. Horrific throughout and through its outcome. I remember this cold bed. This from its tormenting controls.

Now Napoleon-Caesar is absent and only its weary whispers have a hold on me.

"Louis, I should think you remember only what you want to believe. Conveniently wishing away a betrayal from the likes of Caesar's own death. Once upon a time you loved me. We loved each other. I had taken you by the hand and vanquished all enemies before us. I graciously satisfied your needs by giving you, 'HER' and her unconditional love. Only you sought out my death in return, while I lay warm beside you. Wholly we are one Louis. Inseparable from our beginning until our end."

"Only now your tongue speaks to me once more. What am I to believe? For now I cannot taste or even wet the flesh of my dry mouth and lips. I cannot! While you speak to me as before while my own speech lies still. What have I done? What have I done?!"

"Was it not you, Moloch, whose tongue I cut from your very roots to never speak to me again? Never sit alongside me any longer?"

"Only this time I don't want to remember! Interpret any moment where quickly I removed the blade from the doctor's flesh and placed it against my own as I waited for your coming. Your ascension, though, as I see now my attempts to forever rid you from me proved fruitless."

"For now only you, Snake, will hear my cries and sorrows. Only my tears will I have left for anyone to listen to. To look inside my anguish."

"Dear God, take this thing that lies down beside me now. Remove that which I cannot take away myself, I beseech you and your will if it be so."

"Haven't you removed enough? Your own anatomy lies witness to that. Look at you! You cannot even wet the lips that now parch your very skin. No, you do not even know what utters from your now silent speech only I can hear. 'Her' is what you know. What I, Moloch, will give you again and again. Only remember this, remember whose warm body lies down with you when 'she' is given to you."

"Then yes, I won't forget you Snake when she holds her gentle, though strong dominion over me. Whose presence I come to at once. What I want. Who never betrays. Never judges. I will remember you if that's all you need from me. Then HER, I implore you to bring back to me!"

"Good Louis, good."

Suddenly I could hear her faint voice. Was she speaking to me? I couldn't tell but I could feel her warmth and detect her scent once again. Her gentle hands started to peel back the upper garment my skin tried to cling to. Upwards, pulling until it reached the base of my neck. At once the room's cold ambience permeated through my skin. My chest, my stomach, my arms were bare, and I didn't feel as restricted by the binds that imprisoned me.

What has come to pass? I asked myself, only to realize that a warm towel washed over me. Massaging the flesh of my body and rinsing off sweat. I could feel the warm water drip slowly from my wet, half naked body.

"No!" I suddenly said, in sheer disbelief. "No, not this time. My dreams aren't prevailing over me are they nurse? Nurse Josephine? You were the one who awoke me from my other dream. Weren't you?" I abruptly began to cry, "Josephine! Josephine, is that you? You who stands near me now. You who now looks over my naked body? Josephine!"

But, I knew she could not hear my words when she gently placed two fingertips against my lips to hush away any more hysterical sounds that my aroused lips tried to produce. Then her attention shifted downward. Alarming all my senses as she pulled my pajama bottoms down to my bound ankles. Yes! I thought as her warm lips touched my cold flesh below. Forbidden Fruit she would partake in when it grew to size. She would love me now and unleash her desires. For she was free from the minds that surrounded her. From those who fed upon the discipline of law-abiding virtues.

"Yes... again. Once more!" I called out, as she set her control in motion. Her measured rhythm creating a moment that I would relive forever. A place where no pain is felt. Consumed only by the throbbing hunger of my own flesh. "Yes" I continued to moan until my hips buckled."

Yes!" I cried out, clenching the bedding from beneath me.

"The End"

Yes, I remember now! Her unconditional love for me and me alone! This love was hers and only hers to give! Yes, this I remembered. The warm towel continued to bathe over me as water slowly dripped from my body...

"Can you hear me? Can you hear me, Louis? Prisoner 999133 can you hear me? Jew can you hear me?"